Mrs. Henry Wood

The House of Halliwell

Vol. III

Mrs. Henry Wood

The House of Halliwell
Vol. III

ISBN/EAN: 9783337044893

Printed in Europe, USA, Canada, Australia, Japan

Cover: Foto ©Andreas Hilbeck / pixelio.de

More available books at **www.hansebooks.com**

THE
HOUSE OF HALLIWELL

A Novel

BY

MRS. HENRY WOOD

AUTHOR OF
"EAST LYNNE," "THE CHANNINGS," "JOHNNY LUDLOW,"
ETC., ETC.

IN THREE VOLUMES
VOL. III.

LONDON
RICHARD BENTLEY AND SON
Publishers in Ordinary to Her Majesty the Queen
1890

CONTENTS OF VOL. III.

CHAPTER	PAGE
I. A WOODEN LEG	I
II. A SECRET MARRIAGE	22
III. A WANDERER'S RETURN	60
IV. DR. GORING'S SECOND WIFE	88
V. MORE MYSTERY	118
VI. OLD FACES	140
VII. CLARA'S ESCAPADE	170
VIII. SIR THOMAS AND LADY ELLIOT	194
IX. A FORBIDDEN MARRIAGE	219
X. MOTHER AND SON	239
XI. RIGHT AT LAST	273

HOUSE OF HALLIWELL.

CHAPTER I.

A WOODEN LEG.

A SERIOUS misfortune fell, about this time, upon Mrs. Copp. Strictly speaking, it was upon her son, but he did not care for it half so much as she did. The Captain—as he had long been—was with his vessel in the Chinese seas, when it was attacked by a piratical junk. A desperate engagement ensued, and the Captain—we must borrow his own words — "licked the devils into shivers." But alas, though the victory was glorious, poor Captain Copp was wounded in the leg, which was less glorious, for it resulted, later, in its being taken off. He came home, sold his share in the vessel, of which he was part owner, gathered together what other odds and ends of means he was possessed of, the interest of which was sufficient to live upon, and retired from the merchant service. Mrs. Copp spent a whole month in groans and lamentations: it was so heart-sickening to see her fine boy, in the very prime of life, viz., forty years, pegging about upon a wooden leg. Of course he would make his home with her; of that she never entertained a doubt; and when her grief subsided, she commenced various preparations and changes accordingly. Captain Copp rendered them futile. He went a long journey; it was to pay a visit to an old ship-comrade at Coastdown. He fell in love with the little fishing village, determined to establish himself there, and took a cottage off-hand. Aunt Copp was violently wrath, and stormed much, and she went storming up to London, where the Captain then was, buying furniture for his new home. She could do nothing with the Captain as to changing his determination, and she went down and stayed with her nieces at Halliwell House. The Captain occasionally made his appearance by the omnibus; and Mrs. Copp told him to let the furniture-buying alone, and she would see to it. The Captain certainly was displaying all the proverbial wisdom of a sailor in his purchases, securing the most incongruous articles, and ordering them packed and sent off before his mother could catch sight of them, and she looked after him pretty sharply.

"He'll be wanting a servant," said Aunt

Copp one day to Hester; "someone who
can manage for him. He has no more idea
of management than an owl."

"I think I know a young woman who
would suit him. She lived with us more
than three years, and——"

"Then she won't do," snapped Aunt
Copp, who had never recovered her temper
since the Captain first took the Coastdown
cottage. "I am not going to leave Sam
with a giddy young woman. He must have
an old one."

"She is neither young nor giddy, Aunt
Copp," replied Hester. "It is several years
since she lived with us, and she was not a
young girl then. You have heard me speak
of her—Sarah. She was with us when that
affair happened about Mrs. Nash's handker-
chiefs. She left us to be married; but something that Sarah did not like came to light
about the man, and she would not have him.

She has been in service since, but is out of place now."

" Perhaps she would not leave London to live in a nasty wretched fishing hole, that has not ten decent houses in it," grunted Aunt Copp. " No one in their senses would. I wish Sam's other leg had been off before he had gone and found it out."

" I will send and tell her to call here," said Hester. " She is a thoroughly good servant—steady, honest and straightforward. If she has a fault, it is that she is free with her tongue."

" She and Sam will have some tussles, then ; for he won't stand that. But that's their own look-out."

That same evening Sarah came : a most respectable-looking woman, now getting on for forty. Captain Copp happened to be there, and pronounced that she looked a " likely one."

"What can you do?" demanded Aunt Copp, giving her a keen look.

"Anything that's wanted," answered Sarah.

"Now, mother," interrupted the Captain, "let me have the over-hauling of the young woman: she's to serve me, not you. Can you cook a beefsteak, lass?"

"Yes, sir. Broiled, or fried, or in the Dutch-oven before the fire; just as you may like to have it."

"And swab the decks?"

"If that means scouring rooms—yes, I can," answered Sarah.

"Can you wash out a shirt and iron it?"

"I have done plenty of 'em, sir."

"And sewed on buttons?"

"Many a dozen."

"You'll do!" cried Captain Copp. "What's the figure a month? I'm not rich, mind."

"Do!" screamed Mrs. Copp; "you are

out of your senses, Sam. You are not en-
gaging a sailor. A servant's different from
an ablebodied. You have asked her nothing.
Why, if you go to hire servants after that
fashion, you'll get a pretty set about you.
Young woman, are you a particularly steady
character? If not, you had better confess
it; for I could not think of leaving any other
with a young man like my son."

"I don't call this gentleman young,"
returned Sarah. "He looks as if he'd never
see fifty again."

Captain Copp really did. What with his
weather - beaten countenance, its scars, and
his wooden leg, he looked ten years more
than his age. They all laughed at Sarah's
remark—none more heartily than the Captain
himself. Mrs. Copp told her she was mistaken.

"Well," observed Sarah, whom the laughing had not disturbed in the least, "whether

I'm with an old one or a young one, I never
was unsteady yet, and I'm not a-going to
begin now."

" You and your master will be in the house
alone ; there will be no mistress," said Mrs.
Copp, "so you must be up to the management."

" It's all one to me whether there's a mistress, or whether there isn't," repeated Sarah.
" I know what my place is, and the work
that's necessary in a house, and if I'm hired,
I'll undertake to do it."

But Mrs. Copp had a great many more
questions to ask, and suggestions to offer ;
and she then told Sarah to come the next
evening for a final answer, and to settle the
question of wages, intimating that *she* gave
only eight pounds a year to her servant in
the country. The Captain wondered why
Sarah could not have her answer then, and

when she left he pegged across the room with his wooden leg, followed her, and closed the door after him.

" Hello, lass! hi! young woman! here! Don't steer off so fast."

" Sir ?" said Sarah, returning.

" Don't you pay attention to the women-folk in there. They said there'd be no missus ; they'd like to frighten you ; there will be one."

" Then I suppose you are going to be married, sir ?" said Sarah, who generally spoke out what she thought.

" That's just it, lass."

" Well, it won't matter to me," observed Sarah. " I'd as soon serve two people as one ; and sooner, I think, for the sake of more company. We should have been un-common dull, sir, by our two selves."

" All right," nodded the Captain. " She

is not one as will swear at you, I promise that. And, I say" (with a jerk of the head towards the dining-room), "if they want to beat your pay down, let 'em. I'll square it up with you."

The Captain pegged back again, and Sarah departed. She appeared again the following evening, in pursuance of her agreement. Mrs. Copp had been preparing a long string of lectures, which chiefly turned upon morality of conduct, to the extreme amusement of Lucy Halliwell, who knew Sarah was not one to need it. Hester sat apart, sewing, with Amy Zink, who had long been an efficient and patient teacher at Halliwell House.

"I need not remark, young woman," proceeded Aunt Copp, "how necessary it will be for you to keep yourself select, and to yourself. His place is the parlour, and yours is the kitchen. Sailors are particularly loose in their ideas, and with nobody in the house but you and your master, the neighbours will——"

"But there will be somebody else," interrupted Sarah, who had no idea that the information volunteered to her by the Captain was to be kept secret. "There is to be a mistress!"

"Where did you hear that?" demanded Mrs. Copp.

"He told me—master that is to be— when he followed me out of the room last night."

"He meant me," said Mrs. Copp majestically. "But that will be but for a short time, just to get his house set to rights. My home is in Liverpool."

"Oh no, not you, ma'am," replied Sarah; "a wife. He is going to marry."

"He did not say that?" cried the astonished Mrs. Copp.

"Yes, he did," answered Sarah. "He told me I was a-going to have a mistress, but I needn't be afeared, for she was not one as would swear at me. So I asked him outright whether he meant that he was a-going to take a wife, and he said yes, he did mean it."

What Aunt Copp's wrath might have brought her to, it is impossible to say, for she fully believed this to be an invention of Sarah's to escape further lecturing; but at that moment Amy Zink threw her hands up to her face, and burst into hysterical sobs.

"What on earth's the matter now?" cried Aunt Copp, turning round.

"Amy," cried Lucy; "Amy! Are you ill?"

Amy sobbed on, emitting also sundry moans and ejaculations; and Hester, after a few moments, seemed to understand. Perhaps she had been more observant than the others ; her suspicions had once been half aroused.

"Amy," she said, "compose yourself. Samuel has asked you to be his wife, has he not ?"

"O-o-o-o-h !" groaned Amy. "Don't be angry with him, please ! Don't turn me out !"

"Has he asked you ?" quickly added Lucy.

"Yes, he has !" returned Amy, sobbing until she choked. "Indeed, Mrs. Copp, I'll do everything for him ! I'll serve him every minute of my days. Indeed, Miss Halliwell, Miss Lucy, I never *thought* of such a thing as his choosing me till he had done it, and then I trembled so I couldn't believe my ears. It was last Sunday afternoon, when the servants were out, and you sent me into the kitchen to show him how the new cooking-range acted. Oh! what shall I do?"

Aunt Copp sat down, completely cowed. Never had Sam taken so iniquitous an advantage of her. The settling himself at Coastdown was play compared with this.

When he appeared the next day, she attacked him violently, and asked how he came to do it.

"Well," answered the Captain equably, "it occurred to me that I might as well splice with somebody before I went down there, and I thought she'd do as well as another. And a sight better than some; for, let me blow off as sharp as I will, she's not one to blow back again."

"Why, she's older than you!"

"Don't know anything about that," answered the Captain, "and don't care.

Very like she may be ; but she doesn't look as old as me, by one half. Oh, we shall do, mother !"

Aunt Copp went back forthwith to Liverpool, in dreadful dudgeon, and Captain Copp fixed the day of his marriage with Amy for a quiet morning at the neighbouring church. The day before the wedding, Miss Oldstage called at Halliwell House with Thomas and Jessie Pepper, Thomas a growing youth, with a round face and a colour. The children were orphans now, Colonel Pepper having died in India the previous year. They were left very well off. Miss Oldstage stayed to dine and take an early tea, and they were about to depart when Captain Copp, who had come in, gave an unceremonious invitation to young Tom Pepper to stop and attend his wedding on the morrow. Tom was immediately wild to do so, and said his Aunt Priscilla and Jessie might go home without him. So it was settled that he should remain for the night.

"What are you to be, Tom?" asked Lucy, when his aunt had left.

"I am to be a soldier," answered Tom. "It is decided."

"What! go into the army?"

Tom nodded his head in glee.

"I am very sorry, then, Tom," said Lucy. "You may get shot."

"Papa did not," answered the lad. "And think of all the engagements he was in, Aunt Lucy; especially those bloody battles of the Punjab. Wasn't Chillianwallah a stunner for slaughter?"

"Miss Oldstage says she has talked herself hoarse, striving to persuade you to be a minister," continued Lucy.

"Do you know why she wants me?" answered young Tom. "There's a fellow always going there when my guardian's out — a thin scarecrow of a Methodist parson—and he's trying to persuade Aunt Priscilla to desert church, and to go to that little round chapel of his, which he calls Jecoliah."

"For shame, Tom!" interrupted Lucy, putting on a grave face, while Captain Copp slapped his leg in ecstasy.

"Aunt Priscilla tells him she shall never turn round from church on a Sunday ; but she goes to his chapel sometimes on the week-day prayer meeting evening. She took me and Jessie one evening. My! you should have heard the singing! It gave us both the stomach-ache."

"Tom," interrupted Lucy again, "I will not hear you speak against any religious sect, whatever they may be. It is very wrong : it is like making a joke of religion."

"I don't speak against religion, Aunt

Lucy," interrupted the boy; "I know that is wrong; but I shall speak against that Brother Straithorn. He is always worrying Aunt Priscilla to make me a minister—Sparkinson says it's because he'd like to get the training of me. And I don't speak against him because he is a Methodist parson, but because he's an old hypocrite, and I know he is."

"How do you know it?"

"I'm sure of it," logically answered Tom Pepper, "and Gus Sparkinson knows it too. He's a sneak, that's what he is. He comes sneaking to the house when my guardian, Uncle Pepper, is out, but he dare not show his face there when he is at home. I don't like sneaks."

"Nor I, Tom," said the sailor. "Is your uncle kind to you?"

"Very. Rather stiff and particular; but then you know he is old. He was a great many years older than papa. And Aunt Pris is three years younger than papa."

" What brings her name Oldstage ?" cried Captain Copp. " I forget all about it. Why isn't it Pepper, if she is their sister ?"

" The mother was married twice," explained Lucy. " On her first husband's death, she married a Mr. Oldstage."

" My guardian wants me to go into his bank," continued Tom. " But I can't, for I'd rather be a soldier than anything in the world."

" Stick to it, lad," cried Captain Copp. " My father wanted me to be anything but a sailor, but I couldn't be persuaded. I had a sailor's craft in my head, and you have a soldier's."

" Papa directed, in his will, that I was to be allowed my choice of a profession," added Tom ; "so Aunt Priscilla and Brother Straithorn can't do me out of it."

The following morning rose, and the
wedding was as quiet as could be. Tom
Pepper and Lucy (who put off her deep
mourning for the day) went to church with
them, and a seafaring friend of the Captain's,
named Luttrell. The two Captains, when
they appeared, both having come down in a
coach together, proved to be dressed exactly
alike, in blue coats and trousers, crimson
waistcoats and sea-green neckerchiefs, tied in
a sailor's knot. The coachman had been pre-
sented with a bunch of sea-green streamers
for his button-hole. The same coach took
them to church. Captain Copp (out of some
wrong-headed idea of politeness, he having
been its hirer) obstinately persisted, both in
going and returning, in putting the four
others inside, and mounting himself and his
wooden leg on to the box beside the driver,
to the timid confusion of Amy and indignation of Lucy, who remonstrated with him in

vain. Tom Pepper was for mounting the roof, but Lucy did overrule that.

So Captain Copp's nuptial knot was tied, and he and his wife Amy left for Coastdown, where Sarah had preceded them.

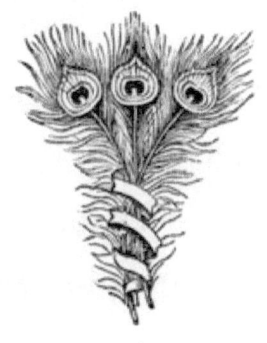

CHAPTER II.

A SECRET MARRIAGE.

AUNT COPP had once prophesied that Hester's life would be full of business and care, and it really seemed like it. They had but just got Captain Copp's wedding over, when a letter arrived from Mr. Halliwell at Chelson, saying that his wife (who had long been in a poor state of health) was worse than usual, and begging Hester to go there.

"What is to be done, Lucy?"

"I do not see how you can refuse to go," was Lucy's reply. "Poor Alfred! what trouble and worry he has! And the very last man formed by nature for a life of care."

" Don't say that, Lucy," remonstrated Hester; "to us he seemed so; but, rely upon it, the back is always fitted to the burden. It may be that had Alfred been more favourably circumstanced, he would have led a life of dreamy, useless indolence —have kept a curate to do the work, and shuffled off action and responsibility from himself."

Hester wrote an answer, and started for Chelson on the following Monday. The rail conveyed her thither in a few hours, and she got out on to the platform. She was looking out for her trunk when a boy who appeared to be one of the employed, and was busy with the porters, ran up to her :

" If you please, are you Aunt Hester ?"

She was taken by surprise. Could it be

that one of her brother's boys was working
at the railway-station? "Who are you?"
she asked.

"I am Sam, Aunt Hester. Next to Tom.
Shall I see to your luggage?"

"Yes, my dear. I will walk on."

"The omnibus will go round the town
directly. Papa told me to put you in it."

But Hester preferred to walk, Sam calling
after her to ask if she knew her way. She
remembered it quite well, reached the house,
and knocked. The door was opened by a
flaunty-looking servant, with open sleeves
and a piece of round white lace stuck on the
back of her head. Hester wondered if she
called it a cap.

"Is Mr. Halliwell at home?"

"Mr. Halliwell!" was the answer. "What,
the parson?"

"Yes. The Reverend Mr. Halliwell. Is
he at home?"

" He don't live here, mum.   He lives at
the Vicarage."

" At the Vicarage !" repeated Hester in
her surprise.

" Yes, he do," was the girl's answer.   " He
have moved into it, out of here, this two
years."

Hester turned towards the Vicarage, with
an oppressed feeling at her heart.   To think
that they should have gone back to that
terrible place, where, as Mabel had once
observed to her, the wet ran down the walls
and the odours made her ill.   Her brother
was standing at the churchyard steps.
Strangely altered ; bowed, and gray and
broken ! in appearance an old man, though
not yet fifty.

" Are you walking, Hester ?" he exclaimed.   " I told Samuel to put you into
the omnibus."

" My legs were cramped with the journey,"

she replied, as he took her hand. "How is Mabel?"

"Better to - day. It is the thought of your coming. I fear, Hester, we shall lose her."

"Alfred," she exclaimed, almost passion-ately, "what brings you back, living at this unwholesome place?"

"There was no help for it," he sadly said. "Expenses were so heavy upon me, I was unable to pay rent."

Unconsciously Hester had halted, leaning with her elbow on the low gate of the church-yard. Her heart was full. "I did not know Samuel," she observed.

"I dare say not. He was a little chap in petticoats, I suppose, when you were last here."

"I mean I never should have looked out for him as one of the railway servants. I do not speak in any spirit of false pride, Alfred, but it vexed me to see him there, the son of a clergyman."

" I cannot do better," replied Mr. Halliwell. " Perhaps in time something may turn up. I strove to keep my boys to occupations only fitted for gentlemen. I was in hopes, great hopes, of sending George to college—in a subordinate capacity, of course ; what we call a servitor; and I kept him at home to his reading and his classics. But one cannot confine boys of seventeen indoors, and always have an eye over them. I am obliged to be out much, and it seems George used to get out. He made acquaintance with expensive companions ; they led him into debt, and it nearly ruined me."

" Debt which you had to pay ?" asked Hester.

" Yes. It was almost sixty pounds. I thought every stick and stone we had must have been sold. But they gave me time, and are giving it me still."

"And where's George now?"

"That's the worst part of the business. It is that," he added, lowering his voice, "which has brought down his mother. He had as good a heart, poor fellow, as ever breathed, and when he saw the embarrassment his imprudent thoughtlessness caused, he started off, saying he would no longer be a source of grief to us, and went to sea."

"To what part of the world? When did you hear from him?" reiterated Hester.

"Never since," he whispered, turning away his face, so that Hester could not see it.

"Why, can that be Sam! wheeling down my luggage himself!" uttered Hester.

Mr. Halliwell looked towards the advancing truck. "Yes, it is Samuel," he quietly said, not seeming to feel the affair in the least.

"Samuel, how could you think of doing such a thing!" Hester exclaimed when he came up. "I told you to let the omnibus bring my boxes."

"The omnibus would have charged you a shilling, Aunt Hester," returned the boy, looking at her with a good-humoured smile on his bright face: "sixpence for the trunk, though it is small, and sixpence for the band-box. It has not hurt me."

"Well, Sam, as you have done it, and it can't be helped, there's the shilling for you."

"Oh no, indeed, Aunt Hester, I did not do it to get the shilling for myself. That would be cheating the company ; but, of course, as you are my aunt, I could bring them free if I liked. I will not take it, thank you."

"Very well," said Hester, admiring the lad in her heart. "If young porters are too proud to accept shillings, I cannot help it."

"Better for him to be at this honest

employment, though he is the descendant of a race of·gentlemen, if it keeps him out of mischief, than go wrong through idleness, as George did," whispered Mr. Halliwell to his sister.

"Yes, yes, Alfred, it is better. What is Tom doing ?"

"Thomas is in his Uncle Zink's office."

"Articled ?"

"Only as a clerk," sighed Mr. Halliwell. " He gets a trifle a week. We cannot place boys out as gentlemen, Hester, without premium, nowadays ; and I have not got it to·pay."

At the door of the Vicarage stood Emma and Annie, both lady-like girls, and one of them, Emma, extremely pretty. Though only attired in cheap alpaca dresses, they looked like the daughters of a gentleman. Archibald, the youngest child, was peeping out of the parlour.

"Now guess which is which," said Mr.
Halliwell.

Hester looked at the smiling, blushing
countenances of the two young ladies, and
guessed wrongly. " That is Annie," she
said, pointing to the pretty one, with the
rich colour and merry eyes. Mr. Halliwell
laughed.

" This is Emma. Lead your aunt upstairs
to your mamma, children."

Hester followed them to Mrs. Halliwell's
bed-chamber, the very room from which she
had stolen the ornamental bands that Sacrament Sunday so long ago, and the occurrence
came forcibly to her mind as she crossed the
threshold and saw the dressing-table whence
she had taken them. The room looked very
nice : the curtains, sheets and dressing-cloths
snowy white. Mrs. Halliwell was sitting up
in bed, sewing, her thin face as white as the
linen.

"Mamma, here is Aunt Hester."

The pink hectic flushed into her face then, and her trembling hands let fall the work. Hester leaned over the bed and kissed her. "You look poorly, Mabel," she said, "but I have come to cure you."

"You have come to see me die," she whispered; and there was a resigned expression in her face which Hester had never before seen in it.

Hester took off her shawl and bonnet and sat down by her, and the two girls left the room, to get tea ready, by their mother's orders.

"How have you managed to get into this weak state?" inquired Hester.

Mrs. Halliwell did not answer immediately, but lay with her handkerchief pressed to her face—Hester thought to hide the tears.

"It has come on by degrees," she said: "I have had *so much* to bear. But I am not grumbling as I used to do," she hastily added, as an earnest, happy expression flitted over her countenance. "Oh, Hester! how I could have gone on for all those years without LIGHT coming to me, I cannot tell. Do you remember how I would abuse and despise Alfred for that welcoming of trouble, that resigned, *trusting* spirit of his?"

Hester nodded.

"But it came to me also in God's own good time. I see things clearly now; I did not then. Trials, troubles as we call them, are sent to us in mercy, and accordingly as they are received, they are to us miseries or blessings. Alfred, in his submissive, trustful spirit, made them the former; *I* murmured and rebelled. But, as I say, light has come to me; and I can look back now on my life of care, and truthfully say I would not change its remembrance for that of an easier one."

" Then you are happy, Mabel ?"

" Quite happy," she answered, with a movement of the hands which spoke perfect content. " When the conviction first stole upon me that I was declining, I could not have said so, on account of my children. For myself I had no regrets, for I had found my Saviour ; but oh ! to leave my children ! To feel that I was going to be taken to a heavenly home, and that they—perhaps one, perhaps two—more—how could I tell ? might never come to it ! that no mother would henceforth be with them, to be their guide, and whisper a warning, a word in season, or to pray for them ! and then a remorse came to me : that when they were young I might have done so much more than I did do, to turn their hearts and hopes heavenward. But all that anguish has passed—save for one of them—and I am content to leave them in the hands of HIM who has drawn me to Him, and will, I surely trust, in due course, draw them also."

" How long have you been ill?" inquired Hester.

" It is a long, long time since I felt strong; but I have been palpably declining nearly two years. There is not much the matter with me, even now, beyond want of strength."

" Have you a good appetite?"

" Not now, and it has been very dainty throughout. Delicacies, niceties, I could have eaten; indeed, I used to crave for them with an intense longing: fowl, and tender cuts out of a large joint of meat, and strong beer, and similar things. But of course we could not procure them, and our common food I was unable to eat. I expect that has been the chief cause of my decline, a want of proper nourishment. Since it has been known that I am seriously ill, everyone is very kind, sending me jellies and wine and tempting bits from their own table; but the craving for them is gone, and they do me no good. Did Alfred tell you about George?"

" Yes."

" Oh, if I could but see him! if I could but know where he is! if I could but have him with me for an hour, here, by my bedside, and charge him to struggle through life, bearing one end in view—to come to me *up there*—it seems that I could die in peace!"

She had pointed her hand to the sky as she spoke, and Hester could not trust her voice to speak just then.

" Two years," she continued, " two whole years and never to have heard of him! whether he is dead or alive, whether he is in distress ; in slavery; whether he is with companions that will lead him into all evil. Oh, Hester! and he was my first-born, my dearest child."

" He is in God's hands," whispered Hester. " And, Mabel, so are your cares."

" I know it, I know it. But for that know-
ledge I scarcely think I could bear the care
for him which presses on me.   Oh, George !
my boy, my boy !   I often wish, Hester, he
had gone before me, a child, as poor little
David did."

"And so old Betty is dead," observed
Hester, .by way of diverting Mabel's sad
thoughts.

" Betty is dead.   There lies another of my
regrets : I never appreciated her as I ought.
She had so hard a life here, yet I made little
effort to smooth things for her, but too often
found fault and grumbled.   She stopped with
us, good faithful creature, as long as she
could stop, faring hardly and never asking for
her wages.   She is better off now.   Hester,
tell me all the particulars about your ill-fated
sister, Mrs. Goring.   Alfred and I cannot
understand her death yet."

" I will tell you to-morrow, Mabel, not this

evening. It is a long tale. Were you not surprised at Amy's marriage?"

Mrs. Halliwell could not help smiling. "Indeed we were surprised at both of them. At him for choosing Amy, so meek and retiring, and at her for putting up with a husband who had a wooden leg. I do not see why they should not be very happy. The worst is Mrs. Copp's displeasure. Do you think she will ever be reconciled?"

"She is reconciled already," laughed Hester. "Have you not heard it from Amy? She went off to Liverpool in the height of displeasure; but, before the Captain and Amy had been at home a fortnight, who should arrive there but Aunt Copp, with two chests of linen as a present, and a silver tea-pot."

"Then she is with them now?"

"And no doubt will be till Christmas," added Hester.

" Mamma," said Annie, looking in, "tea is ready. Are we to bring Aunt Hester's up with yours, or will she come down into the parlour ?"

" Bring it up," said Hester.

" No, no," interrupted Mrs. Halliwell. " I must not monopolize you entirely ; what would Alfred say ? Go down and have your tea with him, and come up to me again afterwards."

Before Hester had been many days at the vicarage, it struck her that the two girls had some secret between them. Upon going into a room she more than once surprised them in a whispered conversation, and at the sight of her they had started from each other like detected criminals — their faces turned crimson. However, she attached little importance to it, imagining it to be some girlish secret. They had but scant leisure. Since Betty died, Mr. and Mrs. Halliwell had kept

no regular servant; a woman went for three
or four hours a-day to do the rough part of
the household work, and Emma and Annie
did the rest. All their spare time was occupied in crochet-work, which they did to sell.
A shop at Camley (an aristocratic village
three miles off) took it from them, and they
earned a good bit of money at it between
them, some weeks as much as eight or ten
shillings. But they did not have it regularly,
there was so much competition for that sort
of work.

On the Wednesday week after Hester got
there, she was sitting in Mrs. Halliwell's
room when Annie came in to ask something
about the dinner.

"Where's Emma?" inquired Mrs. Halliwell.

" She is gone to Camley, mamma."

" To Camley! My dear, why does she
not say when she is going? Your aunt

would have liked the walk with her this fine morning. And why is it always Emma who goes to Camley? You should take it in turns, Annie. You ought to walk sometimes, confined as you are indoors so much."

Annie did not answer, but Hester noticed a very vivid blush rise to her face as she left the room hastily.

" It is a fine morning," observed Hester, "for so late in the year."

" I am sure a walk would do you good, Hester. If you put on your bonnet now you will catch up Emma."

" I should not like to leave you for so long," said Hester.

"Oh, that's nonsense," returned Mabel, with a touch of her old, hasty manner. " You will be back in a couple of hours, and I shall not run away the while. Tell Emma, when you catch her up, that I do not approve of her always being the one to go to Camley and leaving poor Annie at home."

Hester was tempted to the walk, for, excepting to the church on Sunday, she had not been out since she arrived, and she felt that she wanted air. So she departed, and walked fast to overtake Emma; but she could not see her, and at length reached Camley. The shop where she expected her niece to be was readily found, and she entered it; but they said that Miss Halliwell had been and gone nearly a quarter of an hour.

"How in the world can we have missed each other?" thought Hester. However, it was of no use deliberating and streaming about Camley; the only thing was to make the best of her way home again.

Accordingly, she turned back; but, in passing along the village, her eyes happened to wander to the windows over an opposite shop, where grocery, chandlery, brooms, brushes and other miscellaneous articles were sold. Hester stopped involuntarily, for surely she saw Emma Halliwell's side face at that upstairs window! Though it was but for a moment, for the face went back behind the folds of the crimson curtain. Hester crossed the street, intending to knock at the private door and ask for her. But the thought that it might not be Emma caused her to waver; whoever it was wore no bonnet and seemed to be quite at home; she remembered also that her nieces had said they had no acquaintances in Camley. So Hester passed on, and reached home. Emma had not returned. Hester said nothing, only that she had missed her. A full hour afterwards she saw her coming down the churchyard steps hurriedly, her face the colour of a peony. Hester ran and opened the door.

"Emma, you have been a long time," she remarked.

"The patterns were not ready," was Emma's prompt answer. "I had to wait. I thought they were going to keep me in the shop till night."

"There's something wrong here," thought Hester to herself. But she said nothing then—it was not a fitting opportunity.

In the afternoon the equipage of the Reverend George Dewisson came prancing up to the churchyard steps, and the Reverend George alighted from it, walked down them and knocked at the vicarage door. A rare honour; for since his induction to that rich living he had grown more stiff and unsociable than ever. The Earl of Seaford had died within two years of his appointment to it, and the Reverend George had then married. His wife was a lady in her own right; old, and grand and sour; she was one of five sisters, who were all as poor as the poorest mouse in St. Paul's Church ; but he had been caught by the title and had married her.

Mr. Halliwell and his sister received him, and in the course of conversation the former remarked that Lady Lavinia never came now to see Mrs. Halliwell.

" There are—aw " (the Reverend George had talked in a constrained manner when he was curate, and pomposity was added to it now)—" certain rules of society, which—aw— Lady Lavinia, from her position, is especially obliged not to—aw — transgress. She requested me to state, should the subject be led to by you, that she intended no disrespect to —aw—*Mrs. Halliwell* by abstaining from calling."

The words, and the peculiar stress upon his wife's name, puzzled Mr. Halliwell.

" But when—aw—a young lady (as, of

course, a clergyman's daughter must be considered, be her pecuniary circumstances ever
so unfavourable) gives herself up—or, I may
say, in this case, give themselves up, to—
aw—low company : to, in short, an appearance of—aw—bad conduct—it cannot be
expected that Lady Lavinia can — aw —
countenance the family."

Hester blushed for his bad feeling and
vulgar words. If ever the temptation was
strong upon her to tell the world how he had
obtained his living, it was then. But she sat
silent.

Mr. Halliwell's mouth opened with amazement. " Do you allude to my daughters ?"
he inquired.

" I am obliged to say I do. To—aw—the
elder one especially."

" Why, what have they done ?" he asked.

" Report says that they—at least—aw—
one of them, is upon familiar terms, in—aw—

a very familiar sense of the word indeed—
with a man who lives at Camley. Some low
musical fellow of the name of Lipscome, who
gets his living by—aw—fiddling and such
things."

Hester's heart went pit-a-pat against her
side, for she remembered the vision of
Emma's head that very morning, and her
deliberate untruth afterwards. She listened
to the further particulars—rumours, he called
them—entered into by Mr. Dewisson, and
when that gentleman left she laid her hand
on her brother to detain him (for he was
hastening nervously into the room where the
two girls were seated at their crochet) and
spoke calmly.

"There must be some mistake in this,
Alfred. Leave me to penetrate it; the
children will be confused and alarmed if you
question them. You are looking now white
with apprehension. Go out on your after-

noon parish round ; and, above all, say nothing to Mabel."

Hester took her knitting into the other parlour and sat down by her nieces, who had their heads together, as usual, whispering.

" Which of you two ladies is it," she began in a careless tone, " who is upon intimate terms with Lipscome, the music-master ?"

Annie gave a half scream, looked at Emma, and began to tremble violently. She was by far the more excitable and the more sensitive of the two. Emma bent her head lower over her work, and her very neck grew scarlet. Neither spoke.

" Annie," said her aunt, thinking she would question the one whom she suspected to be the least guilty, " are you upon familiar terms of friendship with this Mr. Lipscome ?"

She burst into tears. " No," she sobbed ; " indeed I am not. I have seen but little of him."

" Have you not occasionally gone to his lodgings—where he lives alone ? That is very pretty, I think, for a young lady."

" I have never been inside his door," cried Annie earnestly. "It is not my fault."

" What is not your fault ?"

" Good gracious, aunt," interrupted Emma testily, "if we have spoken, once in a way, with Mr. Lipscome, where's the harm of it ? Papa and mamma would like to keep us curbed up, like mice in a trap. Don't make yourself such a simpleton, Annie : there's nothing for *you* to sob over."

" There is a great deal of harm," returned Hester in stern tones, for the girl's careless words provoked her. " A communication has been made to your father that you have acted so as to raise serious reports against your fair name. It is not possible that you, a clergyman's daughter, carefully brought up, can have conducted yourself so as to deserve them."

"Oh, Emma," implored Annie, in deep agitation, "tell the truth. You know it cannot be hidden always. Tell Aunt Hester: perhaps she will break it to papa."

Hester's flesh was creeping all over: she hardly knew what dreadful thing to fear. It did not creep less at Emma's next words.

" *Will* you stand between me and papa's anger, Aunt Hester? I know it is very bad, but it is done."

"What is done?" breathed Hester, hardly able to get the words from her dry lips.

" I am married," she whispered.

Hester sprang from her chair. " Married!" But the word was a relief in that moment of wretched suspense. Then came the thought, was she wilfully deceiving her, or was she deceived herself? For how could a girl go through the ceremony of marriage in a country place without her father being cognisant of it, and he a clergyman?

"Do you doubt me?" returned Emma, in answer to her aunt's confused words, and there was a touch of scorn in her tone as she spoke. "We were married in Chelsbro' two months ago, two months this very day. Annie can tell you so. Here is the ring," she added, taking it from the bosom of her dress.

Annie only sobbed; she was in great distress; far more agitated than her culpable sister.

"How could you lend yourself to it, Annie?" her aunt indignantly asked her. "To join in concealing a serious step, like this, from your parents, will be a reproach to you all your after-life."

"I did not know it, aunt," answered Annie, the tears raining from her eyes. "Emma did not tell me for three or four days afterwards. It would have looked like ill-nature to betray her then, when it was too late to prevent it. I have never had a moment's peace since, for terror of its coming out."

"Which church were you married at, in Chelsbro'?" inquired Hester.

"At no church. We were married at the registrar's office."

"Then it is no marriage at all! It will not stand good," breathlessly uttered Hester.

"Yes, it will," said Emma. "Marriage before the registrar is as legal as marriage in a church. I have heard papa himself confess it to be so."

"Marriage before the registrar, indeed!" cried her aunt, in her vexation; "I should be ashamed to think it legal. A barefaced, irreverent way of doing things! You might just as well have jumped over a broomstick. Annie, who is this man? Do you answer me."

" He teaches music, and he plays at the Chelsbro' philharmonic concerts, and copies music ; anything in that way. He has the teaching at Camley ; but that is not much."

" And earns what ?" retorted Hester. " Fifty pounds a year ?"

" More than that, I believe. But still he is too poor to have asked openly for Emma."

" Too poor ! Yet you have wilfully run your head into this imprudent marriage, Emma—this noose of sorrow !"

" Anyway, I shall be better off than being at home," was Emma's answer : and it struck her aunt that her effrontery of manner was only assumed to conceal her desperate un-easiness. " It is nothing, here, but worry and privation ; work, work, work, from morning till night."

" How did you become acquainted with him ?"

" We used to meet him on our road to

Camley, and he took to bowing as he passed us. One day—Annie was not with me—it came on to rain hard, and he spoke, and offered me his umbrella, and walked without himself. We got talking of music. I told him how passionately fond I was of it; that I believed I had a great talent for it, but papa and mamma had never had me taught. Oh, Aunt Hester," she continued in an altered voice, "when I reflect that I might have been trained in that delightful science, instead of passing my days at this horrid employment, or in domestic drudgery, I feel rebellious against everyone! I know I might be earning a good living now, for us all, if they had only let me learn."

Hester could not but feel there was some reason in what she said, for Emma had inherited her mother's talent for music, but in a more eminent degree, and her voice was remarkably fine. "To go back to your explanation," said Hester coldly : " what was the next move, after the day of the umbrella ?"

" I met him again ; I was always meeting him ; more frequently, it seems, when Annie was not with me, than when she was. Then he took me to a concert at the Camley Tea-gardens, and——"

" Took you *where ?*" uttered Hester, in horrified tones.

" They are respectable, Aunt Hester," interrupted Annie. " Very decent people go to them ; not quite the gentry, perhaps. They are about a mile beyond Camley."

" Of course they are respectable," returned Emma, " quite enough so. And I should not care where I went, to hear good music. I went to two. He gave me the tickets."

" And Annie ?"

" Not Annie. She was afraid."

"But how did you account for your absence, at home?" asked her aunt.

Emma hung her head. "I was obliged to make excuses. They suspected nothing, and it was easy."

"Wrong, wrong; all very wrong. And you, Emma, a clergyman's daughter, to have made one at a tea-garden concert!"

"Oh, don't talk, please, about our being clergyman's daughters," retorted Emma, in a spirit of indignation. "Aunt, it is a misfortune that we are so; it is the falsest position anyone can occupy. If we had been born in trade, we should not have had these detestable appearances to keep up, that mamma and Aunt Fanny were always harping upon. You must not do this, and you must not do that, because your papa's a clergyman, a gentleman! And if we had been born rich, we should have received a proper education, and enjoyed amusements, and good clothes, and society.

We may not associate with those beneath us ; and our means (our dress, to go no further) have not allowed of our mixing with our equals, and those above us. We have been denied innocent recreation, for it could not be afforded. Our position has been a wretchedly false one, Aunt Hester, and when the temptation of getting out of it was laid in my way, I could not resist. I did strive : Annie knows I did : but it was too strong for me, that and the prospect of living amongst music ; and I became Edgar Lipscome's wife."

" You unfortunate child !" uttered Hester, in her grief, " what is to become of you ? How are you to live ?"

" He made £80 last year," said Emma. " A great deal more, in proportion, for two of us, than papa's £150, with all its outgoings. Besides, he is teaching me music, and I shall soon be able to help him. It will not take *me* long to master the piano," she added, in a

tone of conscious triumph. " We shall set up
in some large town, perhaps London, and
make a good living. I am not afraid : if
you, dear Aunt Hester, will but be my
mediator with papa and mamma now."

" I do not see much that I can do. The
facts will bear no softening : rebellion, wilfulness, and deceit. Not to speak of the
disgrace to a clergyman's daughter in making
so disreputable a marriage."

" Cler— Now, pray, Aunt Hester, do not,
I say, return to that. It is just rubbish, and
nothing else ; sinful, false rubbish."

Emma's expressive word and tone reminded
Hester of bygone years, when she had heard
the same from her mother, upon very much
the same topic. But Emma was much what
Mabel used to be.

" If it is incumbent on a clergyman's family
to maintain dignity and exclusiveness," continued Emma, " the Church should afford him

pay accordingly. A clergyman's daughter, indeed! I tell you I would rather have been born a blacksmith's — anything. Think of the miserable struggle life has been to papa and mamma! It is sinful—I must speak out, Aunt Hester—it is a sinful system which condemns a clergyman to such toil and privation. Better be a dissenting minister ; better be a Roman Catholic priest."

"Good patience, child!" uttered Hester, when she could give vent to her astonishment; "where have you picked up such words —such notions ?"

"We have not gone through life with our senses shut, Aunt ; at least I have not : Annie is tamer, and puts up with things. The mortifications we have had to bear as your boasted 'clergyman's daughters' would have opened them, if nothing else had. I am glad that the step I have taken will be of some service to my poor father, as he will have one less to keep."

CHAPTER III.

A WANDERER'S RETURN.

THAT night, when all were gone to bed, Hester sat with her brother in the parlour and whispered the truth. Never had she seen him so much excited, so much afflicted. Even his Christian spirit was not proof against the blow.

"Whose fault is this?" he exclaimed. "Can it be called mine? Apart from her own imprudence, her wilful conduct, do you see that blame lies with me and her mother?"

"No; the fault is her own. But *circumstances* have been against your children. The

real blame lies with them, and Emma knows
it. She said to-day she had occupied a false
position in life, and she is right."

It is a painful thing to see a man weep, as
Hester witnessed it in her brother that night.
For the moment, nature had her sway; his
submissive resignation was forgotten, the
bitter feeling, for years so patiently subdued,
was given vent to, and his sense of injury
burst forth as a mountain torrent.

" It is an accursed system ; it must be such
in the sight of God. Why do they leave me,
and such as I am, to toil and starve our lives
out, and lavish their prodigal thousands upon
others of our order, who are no better than we
are, save in patronage ? All the ills of my
life have been brought upon me by this
pernicious poverty. My wife's illness and
early grave, the repression of my children's
spirits, the blighting of their prospects,
George's uncertain fate, and now this last

blow! Look at my own incessant toil, my
broken spirits and health! How dare they
condemn us to a wearing life of labour, exact
from us that we appear as gentlemen, and not
give us the means to bring up and place out
our children! Review what my life and
Mabel's have been——"

It is of no use to record all he said: his
wrongs were strong upon him. But it may be
that had those high in place and power heard
his words, as Hester did, they would have
deemed it incumbent on them to set about
ameliorating the condition of poor clergymen.
Hester gradually soothed him round to the
difficulty immediately before him: Emma's
unfortunate step. How should he act in it?

"It is done, and cannot be undone," Hester
observed. "Scold her as much as you will—
and she deserves it—but see how the best
can be made of it. I suppose it *is* a legal
marriage, as she asserts."

" I shall marry them again," replied Mr. Halliwell, in excitement. " No child of mine shall call herself married upon so irreverent a ceremony."

They sat far into the morning—Hester warning him, when they parted, not to say anything to Mabel that night. Could it have been kept from her entirely, it would have been well; but that was impossible.

Impossible it was found to be. For the following evening Archie managed to betray it to his mamma. Poor little Archibald! he was the errand boy to the family, running and waiting on all, his dearest recreation being to sit by his mother's bed-side. Mrs. Halliwell happened to put a question to him about Emma, and the child's stammering voice and confused countenance betrayed that there was something afoot which she did not understand. She demanded to know.

" I am afraid to tell," answered Archie.

"Archie! Afraid to tell *me!* Speak out, my boy."

"Oh, mamma! Aunt Hester said you were not to be told. I don't know it all myself; I only heard a little."

" You must repeat to me that little, Archie. I will inform your Aunt Hester that I insisted upon knowing."

" Emma has done something very wrong, very disobedient. It is about the music-master at Camley. I don't know, but I think papa is going to marry her to him to-morrow."

Of course these mysterious words were enough to alarm Mrs. Halliwell, and Hester was obliged to break to her the particulars. They shook her pitiably.

" Alfred is going to re-marry them," Hester said.   " He has no option, unless letting the marriage before the registrar serve.   Do not distress yourself, Mabel. It might have been worse."

"Worse!" she exclaimed, "how could it have been worse? Hester, what are you thinking of? The girls have been reared in firm principles. No, no; it is as bad as it can be."

"Alfred marries them to-morrow, and then she leaves with her husband. We sent for him this afternoon, and he came, very penitent. I never saw a man so cowed as he was before Alfred."

"And you intended to keep all this from me!" exclaimed Mrs. Halliwell.

"No," answered her sister-in-law; "how could we keep it from you when Emma was leaving? But we were seeking a favourable opportunity of breaking it to you."

"What do you say his name is?"

"Lipscome. He is a mild, diffident young man, rather good-looking: fonder of Emma

than she deserves, naughty girl, but with not
half her share of sense and firm resolution.
Emma will be master and mistress too."

" Why did he not ask for her openly ?"

" He wanted to do so, as it appears ; but
Emma, and Annie too, thought there would
be no possibility of his obtaining your consent and Alfred's : that a clergyman's
daughter (which, it seems, Emma hates the
name of) would not be allowed to marry a
poor music-master, struggling in his profession ; and she would not let him ask."

Mrs. Halliwell clasped her white hands
together, and lay with her eyes closed.
" The same career of toil for her that I
have had," she murmured, " perhaps worse.
Yet what opportunity had our children of
doing better ?"

" Nay, Mabel, Emma and her husband
may do well," said Hester, for she strove
to make the best of it to the poor mother.

"Both intend to put their shoulder to the wheel; Emma's talents are such as to make headway, and I have heard to-day that he is thought clever in his vocation. And there is one thing, Mabel, which really is a matter of congratulation—he is an excellently conducted man; there is not a taint upon his character. All that might have been worse."

But still Mrs. Halliwell sighed and kept her eyes closed. "Send Emma up to me," she said; "and let me be alone with her."

Hester ran out, when tea was over, to buy some white satin ribbon to put on Emma and Annie's straw bonnets for the morrow, for she really did think it well to make the best of things, especially to the world. She was going along at a sharp pace, having plenty to do that night indoors, when, in turning out of the milliner's shop, she came right in front of three people walking abreast, and recognised the Reverend George Dewisson,

his wife and sister, who were hurrying home
to dinner.   Perhaps the other two would
have passed, but Miss Dewisson stopped.
A regular old maid she was now, a trifle
older than Hester.   She had never forgiven
Mr. Halliwell for marrying Mabel Zink, or
Mabel for marrying him, and the rumours
touching their daughter had not been un-
welcome to her.

"Is it true things are so bad that Mr.
Halliwell is obliged to marry them?" she
asked eagerly.

"They are married, unfortunately, Miss
Dewisson," replied Hester, turning her face
away from the blaze of the gas lamp.   "They
were married two months ago, before the
registrar in Chelsbro'.   That is the greatest
reproach which can be cast at my niece, and
we feel it as a keen one."

"Married before the registrar!" echoed
the Reverend George.   "If that is only—aw

—their own assertion, I should receive it with suspicion, and—aw—doubt."

"We have ascertained the fact to-day, sir," returned Hester. "You can do the same, if you please, for your own satisfaction."

"Why, we heard Mr. Halliwell was going to marry them to-morrow," exclaimed Miss Dewisson. "What stories people tell!"

"You heard correctly. Although legally a wife, my brother does not choose to let her go to her husband's home, really to enter upon her married career, unsanctioned by the rites of the Church."

"That's—aw—as it ought to be," interposed the Reverend George. "Marriage before the registrar may serve for—aw—Dissenters, and such people, but we don't recognise it."

"The affair—though of course most shocking and unbecoming—being less criminally bad than we had been led to suppose, you may acquaint Mrs. Halliwell that I shall resume my occasional visits to her," quoth Lady Lavinia, in a haughty, patronizing voice and manner.

"I will deliver your message to her, ma'am," returned Hester curtly, as she wished them good evening and hurried home.

Hester had been guilty of a bit of innocent subterfuge. Finding the affair of the intended marriage had got wind, she told everyone, especially Tom and Sam, who were applied to as oracles by Chelson, that the time fixed for it was eleven o'clock. But it was at eight in the morning that Mr. Halliwell, stern and pale, stood, in his white surplice, inside the altar railings, and the wedding-party ranged themselves before him. By these means but few people were in the church ; otherwise there would not have been standing room, which would have made an unpleasant crowd for Emma, under the circumstances.

It was not so despicable-looking a wedding-party after all. The bride and her sister were in neat blue and white checked silk dresses, presents from poor Mrs. Goring just before her death, and their straw bonnets and white ribbons looked fresh and well. Hester had lent Emma her white veil of real lace, which, by accident alone, she happened to have with her at Chelson. The boys, called at six in the morning, and informed of the actual hour, were there, dressed in their Sunday clothes, and there also was Mr. Zink, the graceless Tracy of former days. A successful lawyer he was now, as important, in his own esteem, as George Dewisson himself, but very poor, for early extravagance hampered him, and "fast" habits still kept him down. He was there to give Emma away. She and Annie both cried bitterly, Mr. Lipscome was nervous and trembling, and the Reverend Mr. Halli-well read the service somewhat rapidly.

A noise in the church caused Hester to turn her head. Some urchins with their school-books in their hands had come into the aisle, and Jim was driving them out. Jim, as they all still called him, though he had long ago been promoted to the office of sexton and gravedigger. Hester's attention was attracted by a young man not far behind, whose gaze was fixed on the wedding-party with an intensity remarkable to behold. One arm was clasping a pillar, and he leaned forward, with —if Hester saw clearly—tears in his eyes. He wore a rough, large sort of cloth jacket and a blue shirt, like a sailor.

"Aunt Hester," whispered Archibald, who stood next her, and had also looked round at Jim's effort for order: "see that rough man by the pillar. He is so like George."

"Like who, Archie?"

"George, who went to sea. But he was not brown, and his shoulders were not broad and big like that man's, and George was a boy, and that's a man. Oh!"

"Archie, what?" for the child had clasped her hand tightly.

"He is smiling at me. Aunt Hester, do you think it can really be George?"

"I think it may be, Archie."

Just then the ceremony came to an end. The vicar was leaving the altar to lead the way to the vestry, when Archibald, forgetting awe and time and place in this new wonder, went up to his father, caught hold of his surplice, and spoke aloud.

"Papa—is that George?"

"Sir!" was Mr. Halliwell's stern and reproaching reply to the child.

"It is like George, that sailor by the pillar, and I think it is George, because he laughed at me." And there was no longer any doubt, for George, seeing he was recognised, came forward, and was clasped in his father's arms.

"Never comes a trial unaccompanied by a blessing," whispered Hester to her brother through her tears; "this will make up to Mabel for the shock of yesterday."

"Do you go and prepare her for it," he answered.

Mrs. Halliwell was half raised in bed, everything nice about her; for Emma and her husband were to pay her a visit before their departure, when Hester entered the chamber.

"Is it over? Are they married?" she asked.

"Yes," said Hester; "but I will tell you about it when I have spoken of something else. Mabel, I have just made a remark to Alfred—that no trial ever comes unattended by a blessing. You had a great trial to bear yesterday; there is comfort in store for you to-day."

"In knowing that she is married—I mean

according to the rites of religion? Poor Emma!"

"Not that: something greater. Of all earthly blessings that God can send to you, think which you would best love to receive. You have a great surprise at hand."

"The greatest would be to see—oh, Hester! can it be? Is he come?"

"Yes, Mabel dear: George is come; and here; and waiting to come up to you."

She broke out into sobs, and cried like a child.

Emma, with her husband, received her mother's blessing, little thinking it would be the last; and they departed in a fly for Camley. George did not leave his mother's bedside till evening. It was dusk when he came out of the room: for the last hour they had been alone together. Hester, who was in the opposite chamber, saw him, and called him in. He sat down on a low chair, and leaned his head against the bed-post, sobbing.

"Come, George," she said, after letting him give way to it for awhile; "cheer up. Be more of a man."

"I shall never see her again," he said; "never, never."

"That, probably, depends upon the length of your next voyage," returned his aunt.

"No; it does not. If I were to remain, I am quite sure that very, very shortly I should not see her either. In a day or two she will be gone."

"You are mistaken, George. She has been like this a long while."

"Aunt Hester, I think we sailors detect approaching death quicker than landsmen. I have seen instances of it since I have been away. It is on mamma's face to-night, if ever I saw it."

"My dear, we will not discuss it. I

believe your fears mislead you. When must you go?"

"To-night. But if I start at twelve it will do. Or," he added, as if in doubt, "say at one. I could catch it up."

"So soon! What port are you in?"

He mentioned one within a day's walking of Chelson. "I had only leave for a day and two nights," he continued, "and must get back before mid-day to-morrow. It ought to be before eight o'clock; but I'll risk it. I walked here in the night."

"George, the sea is a hard life?"

"Hard!—So hard that I will not describe it to you, Aunt Hester. And I am on a hard ship, in a bad service."

"I am sorry to hear it, my poor boy."

"The next two years may prove better than the two last. At any rate, they can't be worse."

"And what at the end of the two years?"

"Then I can pass my examination for officer, before the Board, and shall look out for a better ship."

"George, is this the life you would have chosen?"

He almost shuddered. "No. Some like it by nature: I do not, even with use."

"Yet you must remain in it?"

"I shall remain in it. When once a fellow has been to sea for two years, nobody on land would give him employment. I shall get along, aunt, in time. It will be different when I am first mate, or captain: I shall like it well enough then."

"George," said Hester, laying her hands on his two shoulders, "in all callings of life there are hardships, and there are blessings. Our care must be to fulfil our duty, whatever it may be."

He nodded.

"Our duty to our fellow-creatures in the

daily concerns of life, as well as our duty to God. Always bearing in mind THE END, and living for it."

"Aunt Hester," he answered, somewhat impatiently, as if not caring to hear from her the precepts he had just listened to from more sacred lips, "I have promised my mother to do my best *for* the end; and I will strive to do it."

Hester took a candle, and turned away to go into Mrs. Halliwell's room, but George spoke to stop her: "Mamma said she would be alone for awhile." Nevertheless, Hester thought she would go in.

She was lying with her eyes closed, but they opened as Hester approached the bed. Her countenance was full of peace—tranquil, entire peace. But—was there a change in it? or was it the shade of the candle? Involuntarily Hester thought of George's words. "Mabel," she said, in an indifferent tone, not to alarm her, "do you feel worse?"

"No; I feel better. But I think I am going."

"Oh, Mabel!"

"I was permitted to last till my dearest boy came home: whithersoever we turn, Hester, mercy follows us: and now I can depart in perfect peace. If God's guiding care were not over him, He would not have brought him here to receive my dying admonitions; and I am content now to leave him in His hands—oh, so content!—for I know that we shall meet joyfully, all meet at the Last Day."

Hester ran downstairs. She sent Archie in haste for Mr. Jessup, and then for her brother, who was attending a vestry meeting. Mr. Jessup could do nothing: he thought she was departing, but was not certain. Mabel was certain of it herself, and Mr.

Halliwell went down to prepare the sacrament.

They assembled in her room : the vicar, Hester, and Annie. Annie brought word that Jim was sobbing in the kitchen, and hoping that he might see his mistress once more, so they called him up, and Mabel smiled and held out her hand to him. Poor Jim took it, and only sobbed the more. But there was something Mabel evidently wanted still, as was proved by her anxious glances towards the door. Hester understood them, and, after a minute's hesitating communing with herself, went in search of George.

He was still in the opposite chamber, sitting in the dark, where Hester had left him. " George," she gravely said, "we are going to receive the Holy Communion with your mother. Dare you join in it ?"

"Oh, Aunt Hester ! I am not good enough."

" I can see that she is watching for you
—that your presence there would be her
greatest comfort."

"We sailors do so many things that are
not right, Aunt Hester : we swear, and do
many other wicked things."

" As I fear too many do who are not
sailors ; and the very best of us are but bad.
George," she continued, "none can decide
this question but yourself.   You no doubt do
daily what is wrong, what are sins in the
sight of God.   But you are conscious now
that they are sins."

" Oh yes !"

" And are you truly sorry for them, and
hope that you may be pardoned for
them ?   Above all, do you earnestly wish
that you could be kept from committing
these sins, and that you might lead a better
life ?"

" I do earnestly wish it.   I have been

thinking over, in the dark here, all the sorrow I have caused her, and my heart is ready to break for it. I wish I could be better : more like her."

" Well, George, you know what we must do, and who we must go to, to be made better," was Hester's gentle answer. " I will leave you here for a few minutes by yourself, and then I think—yes, I do think —that you may venture to come in and join us. In the hope, you know, George, darling, that it may give you strength to lead a better life, and to give comfort to your mother. We will wait a few minutes, and if you feel that you can come, do so."

Hester returned to the sick chamber, and soon George came stealing in. Mrs. Halliwell had held out her hand, with a pleased countenance, to Jim, but oh! the joyous grasp, the illumined countenance, with which she greeted George. She drew him close to

46—2

her bedside, and held his hand. The clergyman went up to him.

" Do you feel you may be a partaker of
this ?" he whispered in serious tones.

The colour flew to George's face at the
question, and he glanced at his Aunt
Hester.

" Speak for yourself, George," she said.
" According to the dictates of your conscience."

" I think I may, father," was the hesitating
answer. " I hope I may."

Without another word the minister proceeded to his duty, reading some of the
service for the visitation of the sick, and
then administering the Holy Sacrament.
At its conclusion, Jim returned downstairs,
sobbing still—he was a simple, affectionate-
hearted servant—and the three boys came
up — Thomas, Samuel, and Archibald.
Hester has never repented of the part she

took with regard to the sailor that night, and she believes it was acceptable to One higher than we are.

They gathered round Mrs. Halliwell's bed, and watched her leaving them. One hand still clasped George's, the other had sought her husband's. Poor little Archibald, frightened and tearful, had pushed himself in underneath his father's arm, next to his mother. Her death was one of peace, and so easy that none knew the exact time of the soul's departure. It was a little past twelve.

At one, George left. After he had taken his farewell, Hester went and opened the house door for him, and watched him across the dark churchyard. He flung himself down on the opposite steps, and gave way to his agony of grief, suppressed before the rest. Alas for the trials of life! How bitter at times they are to bear!

Hester remained for the funeral. The Reverend Mr. Dewisson officiated, and a great number of persons attended it, unasked. Half the houses in Chelson were closed, for, if Mr. and Mrs. Halliwell were poor, they were widely respected. On the Monday following, Hester left for London.

"God bless you, Alfred," she said, at parting. "I say to you, as I said to George, bear on to the end. A few more struggles, a little more endurance, and it will cease for ever."

"Hester," he whispered, as he wrung her hand in his with a painful pressure, "forget what I said that night. I was wrong to give way: but the moment's sore anguish betrayed me. I beseech you forget it."

"And do you forget it, too," answered Hester, "for it is not worth remembering. It was no great crime, Alfred."

"Sufficiently great to need repentance. Fare you well, Hester."

And thus she left him to his hard labour and his discouraging poverty. " But I declare," cried Hester, as she took her last look of the damp vicarage, and the omnibus whirled her, in its course, past the luxurious residence of George Dewisson, " I declare that such a state of things is a disgrace to England's Established Church : that the heavy wealth lavished upon some of its members, the wretched poverty of others, is a shame and a sin, and I will declare it to be so as long as the system shall exist, though the whole bench of bishops should convene a court and hang me for it."

CHAPTER IV.

DR. GORING'S SECOND WIFE.

Soon after Hester's return home the school broke up for the Christmas holidays, and Hester departed for Middlebury, according to her agreement. As the account of Mrs. Goring's mysterious death was given in Hester's own words, it may be as well to give this short sequel to it in them also.

I had promised to go down to Dr. Goring's at Christmas, and I did so, getting there for Christmas Day. Matthew and Alfred had come home for their holidays,

and were well, careless, and happy, as it is
fitting schoolboys should be. Mary had
grown, and was much improved, promising
to be as nice-looking as her poor mother.
As to my brother-in-law, he was quite himself again ; had recovered his spirits, and
laughed and talked as before. These gay
natures soon forget loss and sorrow ; and
perhaps it is best they should. One thing
I was glad to find—that he had been prudent
in his expenditure, and was paying off his
debts. Some shares, which he held in a
public company, had suddenly risen to a
high premium : he had been wise enough to
take the opportunity of selling out, and had
realized three or four hundred pounds by it.
This assisted him well.

One morning, as we were seated at break-
fast, the conversation turned upon a friend of
Dr. Goring's, a schoolmaster, who resided in
Middlebury. He had been a widower some

years, but was now going to be married
again to a pretty but portionless girl, and
the town said it was quite a "love match."

" I did not think he would have been such
a fool," observed Dr. Goring.

" In what way?" I asked.

"When a man marries in youth he commonly marries for love, and that's as it should
be; but when he gets to middle age, and
wants a second wife, he ought to look out
for money. Substance, not romance, should
be the motto then."

Somehow I was pleased to hear Matthew
say that, but I did not stay to ask myself
why I was so. And just then the surgery
boy brought in a note.

It was from a Mrs. Poyntz, asking him to
call upon her in the course of the day, as she
was not well. Captain and Mrs. Poyntz
resided about a mile from the town, and
their name brought to my mind the Clutter-

bucks, old friends of mine, who lived in a farm-house close to them. I had not seen these friends for nearly four years, and I began to think, as I sat at my work, that I would go out and call upon them. It was a sharp, frosty morning, bright and cold ; the two boys had gone out to slide, and I pro-posed it to Mary.

We found them at home, Mrs. Clutterbuck in the kitchen making pork-pies ; the well-appointed, roomy old kitchen, where I had once, when I was a young girl, as fond of frolic as the best of them, revelled in all the delights of a harvest-home. Care had not come upon me then. They wanted us to stay the day, and Farmer Clutterbuck (he was always a joking man) hitched my bonnet off, for I was sitting with the strings untied, and gave it to his little granddaughter to run away with and hide. But we could not remain that day, and settled to go another.

It was after one when we left them, and
we set out to walk fast, for we dined at two.
As we turned into the high road from the
lane (Clutterbuck's Lane it was commonly
called, because it led to nothing but their
house), I saw, about a hundred yards before
us, Dr. Goring, walking towards Middlebury,
by the side of a lady.

" There's your papa, Mary !" I exclaimed.
" He has been up to Mrs. Poyntz.   I wonder
who is with him ?"

" It is Miss Howard," replied my niece.

I protest that a cold chill ran through me,
from head to foot, when I heard the name.
How came *she* to be walking with Matthew
Goring ?

" Does Miss Howard live in Middlebury ?"
I asked, when I recovered myself.   For
truth to say, I had never once introduced
her name since I came down ;   I dis-
liked it too much.   "When she left us,

Mary, she was negotiating for a situation in London."

"Yes, but she did not take it," replied Mary. "She has been in Middlebury ever since, staying at her aunt's."

"Sly cat!" I'm afraid I groaned to myself. "She has her eye upon *him*, as sure as my name's Hester Halliwell, and she stays in Middlebury to catch him. What does she do?" I questioned aloud.

"She goes out as daily governess," said Mary. "People say she and her aunt quarrel a good deal."

I went along at a quick pace to come up with them. For I did not like Mary to see her father bending to look into that false face, with every sentence he spoke, as if he were — courting. The word must come, though I hate to write it.

Dr. Goring was surprised to see us : his countenance betrayed it. *She* did not seem in the least discomposed, but greeted us with a flow of words in her modulated voice.

" We shall be late for dinner, Matthew," I observed ; "we had better get on."

He drew out his watch and looked at it. " Not at all late," he said.   " It is only half-past one."

He did not seem inclined to walk faster, or to quit her side, and I did not choose to leave him in her society.   So we slackened our pace to theirs ; and thus it happened that we were seen walking into Middlebury, side by side with that woman, who may have been the author of Mary Goring's death.

She turned off to her aunt's before we reached our street, and then I asked my brother-in-law whatever brought him walking with Miss Howard.

" I overtook her as I was returning from Mrs. Poyntz," he replied, "just before you came up with us."

I could not say anything to this, for I had no right to dictate to Matthew Goring whom he should, or should not, join in a walk, and talk to ; so I held my peace. But I know I was very cross at the dinner-table afterwards, scolding Alfred for upsetting the gravy upon the table-cloth—and the next minute I my-self upset some ale.

When the holidays had expired, Matthew and Alfred went back to school, and I returned home. I did not go down again at Midsummer, for a pupil from India, of whom we had entire charge, was falling into delicate health, and the doctors ordered the seaside for her. So my sister Lucy, who was like-wise wanting a little change, accompanied her to Ramsgate with Frances, and I stayed at home to take care of the house and the other pupils, five or six of whom generally remained the holidays with us.

We had resumed school about a fortnight,

when I received a letter from Middlebury, from Mrs. Tom Halliwell. The following passage was in it: " Rumour says that Dr. Goring is about to be married again, to his children's former governess, Miss Howard."

Had a serpent bitten me, I do not think it could have injured me as did those startling words. They were as I have quoted them, " *Rumour* says," but I instantly felt a deep, prophetic conviction within me that Charlotte Howard would inevitably be Matthew Goring's second wife. Could I do anything to prevent it? What *was* to be done? It was a union that ought not to be—I felt that, in my heart of hearts : a union from which no good could come.

" Lucy," I said to my sister, after tormenting myself for four-and-twenty mortal hours, neglecting my occupations in the day, and tossing restlessly on my bed at night, " Lucy,

I have made up my mind to go to Middlebury."

"But think of the inconvenience, just as
the school has begun, and we with several
fresh pupils!" she urged. "If Matthew
Goring is so obstinately soft as to go and
marry that Miss Howard, of all people in the
world, I should even leave him to do it and
to reap the consequences."

"So should I, if it only affected himself,"
was my answer. "But to give *that* woman
authority over Mary's children! I shall start
by to-morrow's train, Lucy, and you must
manage as well as you can for a few days
without me."

If I could have foreseen that that "few
days" would be as many weeks!

I did not send word I was coming, but
went in and surprised them : pouncing right
upon my brother-in-law in his surgery. It
was getting towards seven o'clock when I

reached the house and astonished Susan. She said Miss Mary had gone out to tea, but her master was at home.

He was busy in his shirt-sleeves (it was an intensely hot day) over some chemical experiment. He held a glass of blue liquid in his hand, and his surprise was so great at seeing me, that, in putting it down, he let some fall.

"Why, Hester!" he exclaimed, "is it you or your ghost?"

"It is I, myself, Matthew," I said, "and very sorry I am to come. Do you know what has brought me?"

"The train, I suppose, and then the omnibus," he replied, with his old propensity for joking.

I sat down on a low wooden stool. There was nothing else at hand, for, of the two chairs, one had a flat globe of glass upon it, and the other a glass syringe as big as a rolling-pin. And I took off my bonnet, and laid it on the floor beside me.

"I had a letter from Mrs. Tom Halliwell a day or two ago," I began. " She told me a bit of news, Matthew, and I have come down to see if it can possibly be true, and, if so, to endeavour to stop it."

" Indeed," he answered. But I saw, by the flush which came to his face, that he knew then, as well as I did, what I had to say : and I saw also that it *was* true ; I saw it with a sinking heart.

" It is said, Matthew, that you are about to marry again."

" I am," he readily replied, as if, in the last minute, he had been nerving himself to face the subject boldly. " When a man is left alone with young children, as I am, Hester, it is a duty he owes them to give them a second mother."

" I don't see the obligation," I answered,

" but we will not contend about that. If he does give them a second mother, an imperative duty lies on him to give them a fitting one."

" Of course," he acquiesced, rather restlessly.

" *Is Miss Howard a fitting mother for the children of your late wife, Mary Goring?* Answer me that, Matthew."

" If I did not deem her so, I should not make her such," he replied, that hot flush on his face growing hotter.

" Oh, Matthew, I could not have believed it of you !" I said, wringing my hands, for my perplexity and sorrow were pressing heavily upon me. " You, with your good sense, with your once deep love for your wife ! You did love her, Matthew."

" Better than I shall ever love another, Hester," was his impulsive answer ; " with a different love. We do not marry a second wife—in our advancing age—with the feelings with which we wed a first. And no second wife need expect it."

" Well, I did not come all the way down here to talk sentiment," I grumbled. " The whole world lay before you to choose from ; the whole world : *how* could you choose Charlotte Howard ?"

" Why not choose her, as well as anyone else ?"

" *Why not choose her ?*" I looked at him in astonishment. " Has she bewitched you, Matthew Goring ? Has she taken away your proper sense—thrown dust in your mind's eyes—deadened all decency of feeling ? A woman whose hands may be stained with the deepest known crime, who was probably the destroyer of Mary Goring !"

" Hester, hold your peace," he authoritatively interrupted, rising in anger from off the table, where he had perched himself. " I will not permit you to give utterance to ideas so disgraceful. How dare you couple Miss Howard's name with that of murder? If I were not sure that she is innocent of this, and any other sin, do you think I would attempt to make her my wife?"

"Do you remember what you once said about a man being a fool to marry, at your age, for love?"

"No, I don't remember it," he doggedly replied. "But if you suppose I am over head and ears in love with Miss Howard, like a green schoolboy, you are mistaken. Though I think her a very charming young woman, there's many another I should like for my wife, just as well as Miss Howard."

"Then why on earth do you marry her?"

"I hardly know how it came about, Hester. I have been with her a good deal lately—had got into *the habit* of being with her; and one evening, in a merry mood, I popped the question. I declare to goodness, the words were no sooner out than I thought myself an idiot for my pains. Now you know as much about it as I do."

"You had better have popped it to me," I wrathfully answered, not caring what I said in my anger; and Matthew laughed.

"Because you would not have taken advantage of it. Well, she did, and the thing's settled, so let us have done with it. But don't go fancying again that I'm spooney upon Miss Howard. When a man's turned forty," he went on, laughing, "it is a cut-up to his dignity to believe him susceptible of that kind of nonsense."

"How can you have been so dreadfully blind, Matthew?" I ejaculated. "Blind to your own prospects and happiness?"

"Do you mean as to her want of money?"

"No. But a woman capable of flirting, as

she did with you, in your wife's lifetime, will flirt with others when she is a wife herself."

"I think not," he answered. "When once these women who are getting on in life marry, they sober and settle down. It is only the sting of neglect that causes them to covet unlawful admiration."

"Matthew," I said, rising from my hard seat, "can *anything* I may say induce you to put aside this marriage? I ask it for your daughter Mary's sake."

"Nothing," he returned. "I have made up my mind about it, and the marriage will be carried out. My word and my honour are pledged."

"Had you any idea during my sister's life-time—— Stay," interrupting myself, "I won't say that, for I do not think of you so ill; I will say at the period of Mary's death, and immediately after it, did the thought or wish cross your mind, then, of putting Miss Howard into her place ?"

"Never ; so help me, Heaven !" he earnestly replied. "Indeed, I took rather an antipathy to Miss Howard just then, in consequence of what you said, Hester, that her propensity for flirting with me, or mine with her, or both, had given pain to Mary. If someone had flown away with Miss Howard into the moon, and kept her there, I'm sure it would not have caused me a regret, or a passing thought."

"Yes ; your conduct together embittered the concluding months of your wife's lifetime," I uttered to him ; "and mark my words, Matthew Goring, *no good to either of you will come of this marriage.* I do not allude to any suspicion of a darker crime in saying this : let that lie between Miss Howard and her conscience ; but when a woman has stepped between man and wife — has perseveringly

set herself out to ruin their wedded happiness, and held at naught the work of God,
who brought them together — no blessing
can ever rest upon a future union of that
husband and that false woman. No blessing,
no luck, Matthew Goring, will attend yours
with Charlotte Howard."

I left the surgery, and went about the
house, and found he had been making preparations for his new wife. The drawing-
room was newly papered and painted, also
his bed and dressing room. The old ward-
robe, with one wing, had been taken out, and
was replaced by a large, handsome new one ;
and there was a full-length swing-glass, and
other new and expensive articles, which my
poor sister had never possessed, and perhaps
never felt the want of. This is often the
case with a second wife, I have observed—as
if men would make up in attentions what
they cannot give in love. As I was looking

round the room, Susan came in to turn down the bed.

"You have some new furniture here, I see," was my observation to the girl.

"Yes, ma'am. What with the white-washers, and painters, and paperers, and these new things coming in, the house has been like a fair for the last fortnight."

"And what is it all for, Susan?" I went on. Not that it is my general habit to gossip with servants.

"Why, ma'am, master has not said anything yet, either to me or to cook ; but we can't be off hearing the reports in the town."

"Well, Susan, you will not gain a better mistress, let her be who she may, than your late one." The tears rose to the maid's eyes as I spoke, and I respected her for that little mark of feeling.

"She'll be no mistress of mine, ma'am," was her remark, uttered warmly. "I couldn't bear her when she lived here, and I'm sure I'm not going to stand and serve her when she's stuck up into my poor mistress's shoes. It's not my place to speak first to master, but when he tells us of the coming change, as, of course, he will do, I shall give warning. I wonder he has said nothing yet."

" Time enough, Susan, I suppose."

" So Dr. Goring seems to think," observed the girl ; " but they say it is to be next week."

" What's to be next week ?" I asked, in tones that must have startled Susan.

" My master's marriage, ma'am. Dr. Ashe's housemaid told me so this morning, and she heard her master and mistress talking of it when she waited at table yesterday. Dr. Ashe is going to take charge of master's patients while he is away on his wedding journey."

" The Lord be merciful to us all in this

world!" I muttered; "and his wife but a
bare twelvemonth cold in her grave! Shame
on Matthew Goring!"

Susan left me to fetch home Jane. She
had been placed (I forget whether I mentioned this) at a school in the town as daily
boarder—going to it at nine in the morning,
and not returning till bed-time, so that she
took her play and walking exercise there.
We had thought it better, when we were
arranging matters after Mary's death. I
went upstairs to see John, but the little
fellow was in bed and asleep. Afterwards I
went into the dining-room, and paced about
it alone, indulging all my trouble.

What extraordinary infatuation could it be
that possessed my brother-in-law? What
did he see in Miss Howard to admire? I
could not tell: I cannot tell to this day; or
whether he saw anything. It is true she
was always after him in the six months she

had lived there (which had been six months too many), with her studied ways, her dark eyes, and her low, false voice. It is astonishing the amount of flirtation she got through in a day, with those apparently innocent manners and quiet voice ; and he had ever been ready to meet her half-way. And my belief is, that if a blackamoor in petticoats, with yellow eyes and green teeth, were to hazard advances, some men would be found ready to make love to her. I once heard it remarked that Miss Howard was a "gentleman's beauty." Perhaps so ; I don't know what their taste may be ; but then how was it that never a one had come forward to secure the beauty for his own property? And what did she really care for Dr. Goring, although she did play herself and her charms off upon him? Not a bit more than she cared for me ; for you may lay it down as an axiom that when a woman has lived half her span of life, her dream of love has long been over. But I think (and Heaven knows I don't judge by myself, though I am an old maid) that when a woman, possessing a vain, worldly disposition, and of no principle, coveting the admiration of the other sex, eager for their society—I think that when a woman of this restless, undesirable nature gets past her thirtieth year, without having been made (or perhaps sought for as) a wife, she grows desperate, and cares nothing what havoc she makes in the happiness of a man and wife. As she cannot boast of a husband herself, she desires, at least, to obtain their admiration in the sight of the world. This had been my opinion twelve months before, when I first found out the intimacy between Dr. Goring and the governess, and this was my opinion of her still.

I asked Mary, when she came in, how it

was I had been kept in ignorance of this contemplated marriage : that it was her duty to have written to me, if no one else did.

"How could I write what I was not sure of, Aunt Hester?" she answered, bursting into tears. "Papa has said nothing whatever to me. But I heard to-day that it is very near."

"So have I heard it, child," I said, walking up and down the room in my sorrow. "Don't grieve, Mary," I added, as she continued to sob. "This is a world full of trials and cares, and God sends them only to win our hearts to a better."

"Aunt Hester," she resumed, stifling her tears, "do I look *very* young?"

"Young!" I said; "why do you ask that question?"

"I wish to go out as governess or teacher in a school; anything of that sort. I have been thinking much about it lately. Only I fear if people know I am but sixteen——"

"My dear," I interrupted, "what nonsense are you talking now?"

"*Don't* force me to live with her, Aunt Hester," she implored, with a sudden burst of feeling that astonished me. "I never can stay here with *her*, and call her 'mother.'"

"Do not fear, Mary," I soothingly said. "Before she puts her foot inside this house I take you out of it."

It was all settled that night with Dr. Goring. I sat up, tired as I was after my journey, till he came home at eleven o'clock, and I told him that from henceforth Mary and Jane must have their home with me and Lucy. "If you will pay us for their board, Matthew, well and good, for you know we are not rich," I said; "but if not, we will still take them, and do without it."

"What ridiculous absurdity, Hester! The girls must remain at home. It is chiefly for their sakes that I am marrying."

"Is it?" I laconically answered; and then I related to him, word for word, the burst of feeling I had witnessed in Mary. He paced about the room, as I had previously done, with his hands in his pockets, and a contraction, as of pain, across his brow. With all his thoughtless folly, he did love his children.

"What is the matter with you all, that you should take this general antipathy to Miss Howard?" he peevishly broke forth.

"Instinct did it with me," I replied; "and a woman, whose conduct with their father caused uneasiness to their dear mother, can never be tolerated by any right-feeling children."

"There you are again, Hester, upon your ridiculous ropes! What could the children have seen of it?"

"Everything," I indignantly answered. "Do you suppose Mary, at her age, was blind and deaf? If I, unsuspicious as my nature is, saw so much in less than a month's sojourn, what must she have remarked who was in the midst of it the whole time?"

I need not pursue the conversation. I won him to reason about the children, and it was settled that Mary and Jane should be placed with me in London. John, who was beginning to go to a day-school, was to remain at home, and Matthew and Alfred would spend their holidays there as usual. Otherwise, the house would be free for his new wife. He offered liberal terms for the girls; he was ever open-hearted; and he also offered to pay for Frances, but I would not accept for more than two. His marriage was really fixed for the approaching week. I was for taking Mary and Jane from the town beforehand, but he said I would greatly oblige him by remaining during the fortnight he intended to be absent, as he did not care

48—2

to leave the house and the young child entirely to servants.

" Matthew Goring," I said, " I would not stay in this house to see you bring home your bride if you paid me for it in gold and diamonds."

" I did not ask it, Hester. You shall receive intimation of my return, and can leave a day previously." And I promised this.

We spoke about his pecuniary affairs. The quiet manner in which he had been living the last twelve months, with the proceeds of the shares I spoke of, had enabled him to pay off the chief of his debts, and the three thousand pounds accruing from his wife's death was intact, and placed out at good interest. He had also insured his own life for two thousand; so that, altogether, things were going on in a more prudent way than formerly. And for this I commended him.

Let no one say they *will*, or *will not*, do a thing, in this world. As St. James tells us, we should add, "If the Lord will." I had affirmed that I would not remain in Dr. Goring's house till he brought home his bride, and yet, when she did come home, there I was. Circumstances had forced me to remain.

CHAPTER V.

MORE MYSTERY.

A FEW days after Dr. Goring's wedding (which you may be sure none of his family attended, though it took place in Middlebury, Miss Howard being married from her aunt's), the little lad, John, was attacked with sore throat and illness. It proved to be scarlet-fever, which was making its appearance in the town; but he had it very favourably, and I would not let Dr. Ashe write to apprise my brother-in-law, lest he should return, in haste, and bring *her* with him. Alas! the next one to be attacked was Mary. The symptoms, in her case, were more violent, and the fever mounted to her head rapidly. I could not leave her; and so, the evening of Matthew's return, there I was.

When the fly that brought them from the railway - station stopped at the door, I happened to be crossing the hall, with a jug of lemonade in my hand for Mary. The man knocked and rang. Susan came flying along the passage to admit them, and I flew away up the stairs. I could not have met her, then, with words of welcome.

" Susan, Susan," I said, calling softly after the maid, "tell your master of Miss Mary's illness; that I am still here; and ask him to come to her room."

I heard the girl open the door; I heard some luggage placed in the hall, and I heard Miss Howard's voice, speaking to Susan. I shut myself into Mary's room, and sitting down on a chair, burst into an agony of sobs, like a child.

I listened to his foot on the stairs, and I stood up and dried my eyes, and tried to look as if I were not crying. Matthew came in. He held out one hand to me in silence, as he turned to the bed where Mary lay.

He stood looking at her, and I stood looking at him. Was it really my brother-in-law, Matthew Goring? Never did I see such a change in any one. He was thinner, paler, appeared worn and haggard, and had a dry nervous cough, which seemed to come from his throat. That a fortnight should have so altered any man!

" Matthew," I said, going round the bed to where he stood, " what is it ? You are ill."

" I have not been well ever since I left home," he answered shortly. " Never mind ; it's nothing. I see Mary is very ill."

" Dangerously so, for the last few hours.

Dr. Ashe has been anxious for you since mid-day."

"Send Susan for him, Hester. I must know exactly how she has been."

There was no necessity to send, for at that moment Dr. Ashe entered. After his departure, Susan came in, and said Mrs. Goring was waiting tea. "Mrs. Goring," not "my mistress." Poor, faithful Susan!

"Bring me a cup upstairs, Susan," said my brother-in-law. "I shall not leave my child. Hester, do you go down."

"I have taken tea hours ago," I replied: "and if not—— Matthew," I broke off, "I expected to have been gone, as you know, before this night, but I could not leave Mary——"

"Thank you, Hester, for remaining with her," he interrupted warmly. "Thank you for all your kindness."

"But you must not ask me to meet your

wife, as a friend and a visitor. I cannot take
my meals at table with her—*her* guest. Do
not be vexed at what you will deem my prejudice, Matthew; I *cannot.* For the re-
mainder of my stay, Susan will bring what
little I want to this room, and I will take it
here."

"As you will," he answered, but in so subdued and mournful a tone that it quite elec-
trified me. Some great sorrow had evidently
fallen on Dr. Goring.

He insisted on my going to bed that night,
as I had been watching the previous one : he
himself would sit up with Mary. It was late,
and I was leaving the room to comply, when
Mrs. Goring came swiftly up the stairs with
a candle in her hand. *She* was looking well,
younger, I thought, than she had been used
to look—her mind, I suppose, was at rest now
—and she was nicely dressed in a blue silk
gown, and wore a thick gold chain of starry-

looking links round her neck, and a watch at
her side. His presents, of course, for she had
possessed nothing of the sort when she lived
there. She hesitated when she saw me, and
made as if she would have come to Mary's
room.

"Don't come in here, ma'am," I called out
in my antipathy ; "you'll catch the fever."

Dr. Goring heard, and, following me to the
door, seconded what I said. "There's no
reason for running into unnecessary danger,
Charlotte. You will do well to keep out of
this chamber ;" and the tone of his voice
sounded, to my ear, remarkably cold.

"I am not timid," she replied, "but I will
do as you wish." And with that, she turned
into their own room, and I heard her bell
ring for Susan to undress her. When she
was the governess she could undress herself,
fast enough.

I could not sleep that night ; I was very

restless.   And once I stole out of my room
and down the stairs, for I slept on the story
above theirs, to look how all was going on
with Mary.

The door was thrown open for the sake of
air, and I bent forward and looked in.   I
remember the scene now, as it appeared in
the feeble rays of the shaded night-lamp.
Mary was lying, as before, unconscious and
tossing with fever, and her father had bowed
his head down upon the bolster beside her,
near to where he sat, and was sobbing—
violent, heavy sobs ; his manly frame shaken
with the intensity of his grief.   I heard his
low moans of anguish, and I saw him clasp
his hands in deep, deep sorrow.   And as I
stood, taking another glance at him, before
creeping back to my own room, an idea
dawned over me that his extreme emotion
was not caused so much by the danger of his
child, as by some tender chord of remem-

brance of her mother, his once dear wife.
Surely Matthew Goring was miraculously
altered !

My niece Mary recovered, but weeks
elapsed before she was able to leave her
room ; and I remained with her. Jane did
not take it. All that time I never associated
with Mrs. Goring, and, beyond some casual
meetings on the stairs, did not see her.
Susan, who consented to stay in the house as
long as we did, brought my meals up to me,
and Mary's when she was gaining strength.
We heard that Mrs. Goring had anticipated,
with much vain gratulation, the period when
she should sit in her new drawing-room
and receive the company who came to pay
the wedding visits. If she had really done
so, she was doomed to disappointment, for
not a soul came near the place ; they were
afraid of the fever. But, as Mary grew
better, her father grew worse : he seemed to

have a continual fever on him; his cough, which had turned to a very bad one, harassed him much, and he was worn to a shadow. His spirits were fearfully depressed; heavy sighs would burst from him; and Susan said that when at meals with Mrs. Goring he would sit and never speak unless she spoke to him. One morning, as I watched him panting in his chair, after one of these fits of coughing, and saw the perspiration on his pale forehead, and marked his laboured breathing, a terrible conviction forced itself upon me that he was not long for this world.

I made some excuse to Mary, ran up-stairs, hurried on my shawl and bonnet, and went out to see Dr. Ashe. I found him at home. I told him the symptoms I had observed in my brother-in-law, his apparent excessive depression and illness since his return, and I spoke of the fear which had that very hour penetrated to my mind, and implored him to tell me what was the matter.

" I really have not the power to tell you, Miss Halliwell," was the reply. " I see how very ill Dr. Goring appears to be, but I cannot fathom the nature of his illness. He never speaks to me of it, though I meet him daily, as I am attending most of his patients for him. It's as much like a neglected cold as anything."

" Is it not a decline ?"

" More a waste than a decline," was Dr. Ashe's rejoinder. " He loses flesh daily. And he certainly seems to have something weighing on his mind."

" And if he continues to lose flesh, and cough as he does, and spit blood——"

" Does he spit blood ?" interrupted Dr. Ashe.

" Susan said so, the other morning. But to resume—if all these symptoms go on, and cannot be mitigated, what is his life worth, Dr. Ashe?"

"Scarcely a month's purchase."

I dragged myself back again: sorrows seemed to be coming thick and threefold upon me. Susan was in Mary's room when I entered it, and said her master was engaged in the dining-room with Mr. Stone, the lawyer.

"Susan says she thinks papa is making his will," whispered Mary.

"Oh, Miss Mary!" interposed the girl, "I did not quite say that. I said that Mr. Stone was writing, and master dictating to him, and that they were talking about wills when I took in the glass that master rang for."

It was an hour after that when we heard Mr. Stone leave; and my brother-in-law came upstairs. I opened the bedroom door, thinking he was coming in, but he turned

into his own room, coughing violently.
When the fit had passed away, I stepped
across the passage and asked if I could get
him anything.

"Nothing. Just step in," he said, pointing to a chair at his side; and down I sat.
"Hester," he continued, "I don't think I
shall be here long, and I am settling my
worldly affairs. I trust you will not refuse to
be the personal guardian of my children."

I could not answer at first; the words
stuck in my throat; but I got them out at
last.

"Do you mean that you have been
making your will, Matthew?"

"Just so."

"I — hope"—I hesitated, and my heart
was beating violently—"that you will not
forget the claims of your children in the
settlement of your property; that you will
do righteous justice by them."

"Fear not, Hester," he whispered, clasping my hand with a hot, nervous pressure—"fear not that I shall forget the interests of Mary's children."

"Nor mine either, I trust," cried a soft, false voice, which made me start from my seat, and Dr. Goring looked round, as Mrs. Goring stepped from the other side of the bed, where she had been hidden by its curtains. "I am your wife, now, Matthew, and as such have the first claim upon you."

"Hester! Mrs. Goring! justice shall be done to all," he uttered impressively. "So far as it lies in my power and ability to judge."

"I beg your pardon, ma'am, for stepping inside here with my brother-in-law," I said, as I shot out of the room. "I certainly did not know you were in the chamber."

However, I had an opportunity of speaking to him later in the day, at dusk, and he told me his plans for his children, but without hinting how his money was left. In every word he uttered there appeared to be a conviction that he should shortly be called from the scene.

"Matthew," I implored, "tell me what is the matter with you."

"I hardly know myself, Hester."

"You seem to have some terrible grief upon you since your return."

"I have had a grief, a sorrow," he replied, "and I believe it has preyed upon my bodily health. I know no other cause for my illness."

"You will surely tell me what it is?"

"I cannot tell you, Hester; or anyone. It must be buried with me."

"If you would speak of it, it might no longer prey upon you."

"Probably not—if I could. But I can't. It is of a nature that—that—in short, it is what may not be spoken of.   I was wrong to acknowledge it."

I was silent, lost in conjecture ; and Dr. Goring resumed :

"One word more, Hester, which will probably be the last confidential one I shall ever speak to you.   At the time of my wife's death, I believe you suspected that I might have been the guilty party——"

"Never, Matthew," I interrupted ; "never for a moment.   I knew you too well.   Where my suspicions did lie, I will not further allude to."

"I am glad you so far did me justice, but I doubted if you did then.   I wished to assure you, Hester, on the faith of a dying man, who must soon appear before his Maker, that I was innocent of the crime, ignorant where to look for its perpetrator. Our babe, who had just died, was not more innocent and ignorant than I.   I would have died myself to save her from it—I wish I had died in her stead. Mary—*my darling!*"

There was a low, passionate wail in his voice as he spoke the name. My heart was aching.

"It occurred to me as I lay awake last night, thinking—I mostly lie awake all night, Hester—that I would give you this, my dying asseveration, lest you should ever have doubted me."

"I never did, Matthew."

He would say no more, I mean as to the cause of his sorrow, and soon, very soon, before Mary was well enough to leave, there came a week of deep confusion and distress. Dr. Goring. broke a blood-vessel; and ere Matthew and Alfred, who were telegraphed for, could arrive at home, he was a corpse. There was no time to send for Frances, so she, poor child, never saw her father, dead or alive, after her mother's death.

We buried him by the side of his wife, in the very grave over which he had been hissed not fifteen months before. Mrs. Goring insisted on following him to it—with unseemly ostentation, it appeared to me, for it was not much the custom in Middlebury for ladies to attend funerals—walking herself next the body, and thrusting Matthew and Alfred behind her. Never mind! never mind! it could not, then, bring her any nearer to his poor heart, or estrange them from it. After they came home Mr. Stone assembled us all in the drawing-room, and produced the will.

One thousand pounds was left to each of the three boys, and two thousand pounds between the three girls. The outstanding fees, when collected, were to be used in liquidation of claims against the estate, which they would considerably more than cover; and the furniture was to be sold, and its proceeds divided equally between the children. The other directions, for their education, etc., I need not mention, but only transcribe the clause which related to Mrs. Goring : " I give and bequeath to my wife, Charlotte Goring, the sum of ONE HUNDRED POUNDS sterling, in recompense of any pecuniary outlay she may have been put to in preparation for her marriage with me."

I stole a glance at her as Mr. Stone folded up the will. Her face was livid, as it had been once before in that room, when I had given her notice to quit her situation in the house as governess, and thought she was looking for something to hurl at me. And its expression—its evil expression ! But it could do no harm now ; and Matthew had, as I truly believed, made his will in the spirit of justice. Mr. Tom Halliwell and Dr. Ashe were the executors.

We went up to London before the sale

of the furniture and effects, which was set about immediately, Mrs. Goring having taken herself from the house in dudgeon the day after the reading of the will.   I took all the children with me, except Matthew and Alfred, who returned to school.   I also took Susan, whom I had engaged as housemaid, for I had grown attached to the girl, and Lucy had written me that one of ours was leaving.   As we travelled up, a lady from a distant part of the country, who sat in the same carriage with us, happened to speak of a Miss Howard who had once been governess to her daughter.   It was a singular coincidence, for I found it was the same Miss Howard, and an irresistible impulse came over me to ask why she parted with her.

"To tell you the plain fact," was the lady's rejoinder to me, laughing as she spoke, "Miss Howard had not been with me long when I found she began to think she had as much right to the society of my husband as I had. So I deemed it well to nip such an illusion in the bud, and discharged her without notice."

Then Matthew Goring had not been her first essay! But I never thought he had, by many. A painful query came into my mind: If *I* had discharged her without notice the day I proposed to him to do so, would those children, sitting opposite to me, now be orphans?

We afterwards heard that Miss Howard— that is, Mrs. Goring—went to reside at a small seaport town in Devonshire. But whether to exert her talents for a livelihood, or to gain one, we did not know. I once wished that she, and all such as she, might do penance in a white sheet; but she probably carries about with her a different penance—her conscience. If so, it is worse than the sheet, for it is a penance that can never leave her by day or by night.

For myself, I am growing sad and sorrowful, and the guardianship of the orphan children is a heavy charge. I daily pray that a greater power than mine may aid me in my direction of them, and I strive to lead them in the right path. My old habit of losing myself in remembrances and conjecture gains upon me. I weary myself with wondering what could have wrought that mysterious change in Dr. Goring after his second marriage, turning him against his recently-chosen wife—chosen in such persistent obstinacy—and leading him to the grave. And his extraordinary will, so full of marked slight towards her; what caused that? Mr. Stone told me, in the presence of the executors, that Dr. Goring gave him no explanation, but was short and peremptory as to that clause. An idea intrudes sometimes : was it by a chance word, on her part, he learnt that she was indeed the wilful instrument of Mary's death—did his mysterious words to me point to that conclusion—and was it remorse for his own blind wilfulness in taking her to his heart that was preying upon him? But, if so, would he not have forthwith put her from him, there and then? It may be thought so. Would he not have brought her to justice? Unless, indeed, some chivalrous feeling towards *a wife* (for he had made her one) forbade it. Alas! if I weary myself with conjectures to the end of my life, I shall never fathom it. The whole matter, from the first to the last, is one of those things that must ever remain in mystery. And I am glad my task of relating it is over, for it has been to me a work of pain.

CHAPTER VI.

OLD FACES.

THE family at Halliwell House were
assembled in the drawing-room one Sunday
afternoon in the Christmas holidays. Miss
Halliwell was seated in her place at the head
of the table, and Mary Goring was opposite
to her, in her Aunt Lucy's seat, cutting
up oranges for the children, the little Gorings
and three or four pupils who were staying the
holidays. They used to like to take dessert
on a Sunday afternoon in the drawing-room,
as it had a pleasant look-out upon the road.
Lucy was suffering from one of her acute

headaches, and sat near the fire in the old armchair of Mrs. Halliwell. It was very grand now, for the young ladies had worked a handsome covering for it. Mary was nearly eighteen now; a slender, graceful girl, far more beautiful than her ill-fated mother had been.

"There's such a pretty carriage at the gate, auntie," cried little John Goring, who was standing at the window.

"Not at our gate, child," said Hester; for they rarely had visitors on a Sunday. Nevertheless, she turned in her chair and looked out.

It was certainly at their gate. A low, stylish landau, with glittering silver ornaments on the horses' harness. A lady in purple velvet and furs was in it, and the footman was ringing at the gate. Presently Susan, Dr. Goring's old servant, came up and handed her mistress a card, saying the lady wished to know if she could speak with her.

"Give it to Miss Goring," said Hester, for her glasses were not at hand, and her eyes were growing rather dim for small print without them. "What does it say, Mary?"

" ' Lady Elliot,' " answered Mary, reading from the card.

"Who is ' Lady Elliot ' ?" exclaimed Lucy. "What can she want with us? Some mistake, perhaps."

"She asked for Miss Halliwell," said Susan. "Shall I show her up here, ma'am?"

"Yes, I suppose so," answered Hester. "But—with these cakes and oranges and glasses about—and the children! Show her into the dining-room, Susan."

Hester followed Susan downstairs, and the lady came in. A pale, delicate woman, with hair quite gray, though she did not look past forty.

"You have a young lady at school with you, a Miss Beale," she began, sitting down away from the fire, and removing the sable fur from her neck.

"Oh yes," answered Hester; "and a dear girl she is. She has been with us five years. But she is not here to-day; she is spending a week with some relatives in Eaton Square. Captain and Mrs. Beale are in India."

"The relatives she is with are friends of mine," returned Lady Elliot; "and I have heard so pleasing an account of your establishment, of the comforts your young ladies enjoy, and the care bestowed on them, that I have been induced to think of placing my daughter with you."

"I am sure we feel much obliged to you," said Hester, in her own simple, courteous way. "If you should decide to entrust us with the young lady, we will do everything in our power for her happiness and welfare."

" She requires peculiar care ; more care and attention than others. But for extra trouble, I should of course expect to give extra remuneration."

" Is she not in good health ?"

"Very good health, robust health ; but " —Lady Elliot suddenly stopped, and then went on hurriedly—"the subject is naturally a painful one to me, and when I allude to it, I am apt to become agitated."

Hester looked at her in astonishment. Her pale cheeks had turned crimson, her breath was laboured, and her hand, as she played with the fur boa she held, was moving nervously. Hester did not know what to say, so sat silent.

"The fact is, her mind is not quite right. Her intellects——"

" Oh," Hester interrupted, speaking, in the

surprise of the moment, more quickly than she might have done, "do not pain yourself by saying more. I fear, if the poor young lady is like that, it would not be possible to receive her here."

"She is not insane," answered Lady Elliot ; "you must not think I have mistaken your house for an asylum ; but she is *silly*. Some days she is so rational that a stranger would not observe anything to be the matter with her ; she will learn her lessons and sew, and practise—for by dint of perseverance we have managed to teach her a little music. Other days she will be childish and silly ; but I can assure you there is no madness, no insanity ; it is only a weakness of intellect."

" How old is she ?"

" She is sixteen. The medical men have recently suggested that, were she placed at school with other young ladies, their companionship and example might tend to

brighten her intellects. My husband is also
of the same opinion. You know him by
reputation, I presume?"

" No ; I am not aware——"

" Sir Thomas Elliot, of —— Square."

" Sir Thomas Elliot, the great physician !"
echoed Hester. "Oh yes, I know him.
Some months ago I took one of our pupils
to him three or four times."

"He is my husband," returned Lady
Elliot. " This child is our only daughter,
and has been a source of great grief to us.
When we first discovered her deficiency, as an
infant, we believed the affliction to be much
worse than it really was ; we feared that she
would be a hopeless idiot ; at least I did, for
mothers, in such a case, can only look at the
worst side. I thought, when the fatal truth
burst upon us, that the shock, the horror, the
grief would have killed me. I fear I loved
the child too much, with a selfish, inordinate

affection : three little daughters before her
had died off, one by one, rendering this last
more ardently coveted, and, when it came,
too fondly cherished. But that hopeless
despair—for it was nothing less—has calmed
down with years ; and though I cannot say
I am happy in my child, I am more so than
I once thought I ever could be. Let me beg
of you to receive her."

The further conversation need not be
related, nor the arrangements that were
entered into. Hester consented to receive
Miss Elliot, upon the understanding that
should her peculiarities prove such as to
draw the attention of the other pupils from
their studies she should at once leave.

The reader cannot have forgotten Tom
Elliot, the random infirmary pupil, or Dr.
Elliot, the physician. He had remained in
Wexborough for some years, after we last
saw him there, struggling on ; then by the

death of Mrs. Turnbull (once Clara Freer) he
and his wife were placed in affluent circumstances.   Squire Turnbull had died early,
and Mrs. Turnbull remained at Turnbull
Park with William Elliot.   The next to die
was Lawyer Freer : he left the whole of his
money to Mrs. Turnbull unconditionally, and
when she died, not many years subsequently,
she left her father's property to Dr. and Mrs.
Elliot, the greater portion of it to go to
William at their death.   A small sum she
secured absolutely to William, to become
his when he came of age.   The Elliots had
then removed to London, and the tide of
luck had set in for Dr. Elliot.   How he got
the name he could hardly have told himself,
but he did get it, and rich patients flocked to
him by dozens and by scores.   The tide still
went on, and one red-letter day Dr. Elliot
was bade to kneel down before her Majesty,
and he rose up Sir Thomas.

Lady Elliot left Halliwell House, and
Hester went upstairs again. She told Lucy
and Miss Goring the purport of her visit—
at least, as much of it as she chose to tell
before the children.

"What made Lady Elliot come this afternoon?" asked Lucy.

Hester did not know, for Lady Elliot had
offered no explanation or apology. "There
are some people who regard Sunday with
little more reverence than week - days,"
Hester observed. "Perhaps Lady Elliot
is one of them."

"I know what our nurse used to say—
that business transacted on a Sunday would
never prosper," interposed Frances Goring.
"And Miss Howard, one day when she
heard her——"

"Don't mention Miss Howard's name,
Frances," interrupted Mary quickly; "you
have been told of that several times."

Frances was apt to be forgetful. Besides, she did not comprehend the full horror which had been brought into the family by Miss Howard.

The second week after the school assembled, Miss Elliot came. Lady Elliot did not bring her : she was ill with a cold ; but, to the very great surprise of Hester and Lucy, Miss Graves did—Miss Graves who had formerly lodged with them. They found she was residing with Lady Elliot as companion, or, rather, over-watcher of her daughter. They scarcely knew her, she was looking so stout and well, but she had aged a great deal and had taken to wearing caps. They had been curious to see Miss Elliot, and found her a short, slight girl, with a small, simpering, vacant face, prominent blue eyes and dark hair.

Mary Goring linked Miss Elliot's arm within hers and led her into the schoolroom.

The pupils were just going in to tea, and Miss Elliot, without the ceremony of being asked, sat down with them, making herself perfectly at home. Miss Graves took it in the dining-room with Hester and Lucy.

"Mrs. Archer is connected by marriage with Sir Thomas Elliot," she explained, "and that is how I obtained the situation."

Her words did not strike particularly upon Hester's mind at the moment, and Miss Graves went on : "I told Lady Elliot how comfortable Clara would be with you, as soon as I heard she had a notion of placing her here—which is but recently, I fancy. The plan seems to have been made up all in a hurry."

"What a terrible affliction to have a child like Miss Elliot!" uttered Lucy.

"Terrible I believe it was to Lady Elliot in the first years, by all I can gather," answered Miss Graves. "She was not the rich Lady Elliot then ; quite the contrary. Sir Thomas was only Dr. Elliot, an obscure country physician, little known or employed ; it is only within these few years that he has come out the great medical star, knighted by the Queen, and run after by every invalid. Many a physician, making his annual thousands, has had to struggle with an early career of poverty ; and Thomas Elliot was one of them. You have not forgotten my sister's husband, Miss Halli-well—the Reverend George Archer ?"

Had Hester forgotten him ! A blush rose to her stupid old face—as she was wont to call it ; though, indeed, everyone knew that it was anything but stupid, or old either— and they might have seen it through the ascending steam as she poured out the tea. Perhaps Lucy did. She quietly answered that she had not forgotten him.

" His mother and this Sir Thomas Elliot's

father were sister and brother. He was a country clergyman."

Here was another recollection awakened. How often had Hester, in those old sunny days, heard George speak of his aunt and uncle Elliot! She had little thought, in her interviews with the renowned Sir Thomas Elliot, touching the health of one of her pupils, that she was speaking with the cousin of George Archer.

"And Tom Elliot—as Sir Thomas, stiff and stately as he is now, was then called—ran away with a young lady, and married her," proceeded Miss Graves. "Her father never forgave them, and left all his money to his eldest daughter; but she, when she died—she died young—bequeathed it to the Elliots. Since then Dr. Elliot has been a rising man."

"He must be an unusually clever man in his profession," remarked Lucy Halliwell. "Everyone says so."

" Not he," answered Miss Graves ; " not a whit more clever than others ; only the run of luck is upon him. He has contrived to obtain the name—to be just now the fashionable physician of the day—and so crowds flock after him."

" Well, he must be a happy man, at any rate," repeated Lucy, " to see himself so successful after his early struggles."

" Not so fast there," rejoined Miss Graves significantly ; " they neither of them give me the idea of being too happy. Sir Thomas is a gloomy, austere man, who seems to have no enjoyment in life ; and no recreation, saving that of giving advice to patients. They say he was a wild, rattling young fellow in youth, whom every lady liked ; but if so, he is strangely altered. And Lady Elliot looks and moves as if she had a continual load of care upon her. I say to myself sometimes that one might as well be in a convent as with them, for they will both sit in the room for hours and never speak. If it were not for Mr. William, I believe they would as soon be under the earth as above it."

" Who is Mr. William ?"

" Their son."

" Their son ?" repeated Hester. " I fancied Miss Elliot was an only child."

" Indeed, I don't know what they would do if they had only her," replied Miss Graves, who had not lost her loquacity, and seemed to speak of the Elliots' family affairs very freely. " Poor thing! what comfort can they find in one afflicted as she is ? Instead of the fond pride that nature urges one to take in a child, there is rather a feeling of shame substituted in a case like Clara Elliot's—a wish that, were it possible, we could hide such a child's very existence from the world. These, I am sure, are Lady Elliot's senti-ments, and I fancy they would be mine.

Believe me, Sir Thomas and Lady Elliot's
hopes and love are confined to their son.
They idolize him."

"Is he older or younger than his
sister?"

"Several years older. He is nearly four-
and-twenty. Ah! and he is worthy of their
love. Very handsome, very fascinating, very
good and affectionate; it is rare, indeed, one
meets with one so deserving of praise as
William Elliot."

"Does he follow his father's profession?"

"No. He is studying for the Bar; and,
report says, likely to shine in it. Not that
there is any necessity for William to work.
His aunt, Mrs. Turnbull, left part of the
property direct to him, and the rest at his
parents' death; and Sir Thomas must be
putting by guineas by the thousand. But
William is as industrious and anxious to suc-
ceed as if he had not a shilling. If I had a

son, or brother, like William Elliot, my pride
in him would have no limit."

Just then Mary Goring came into the
room, and began whispering in her aunt's
ear ; something about Miss Singleton (who
was the head teacher) and bread-and-butter.
Hester could not catch what she said.

" Speak up, child," she said. " We need
have no secrets from Miss Graves."

Still Mary rather hesitated. " It is not for
the bread-and-butter Miss Singleton requested me to inquire," she spoke at length,
blushing, and looking at Miss Graves. " My
aunt always desires that the young ladies
may have as much as ever they can eat."

" Cut thin or thick, as they please," interrupted Lucy ; " but Miss Graves is no
stranger to our arrangements. What is it
you are saying, Mary ?"

" We only feared Miss Elliot might make
herself ill," resumed Mary. " She——"

"What! has she one of her eating fits upon her?" sharply interrupted Miss Graves. " Is she eating a great deal ?"

" Fourteen slices since we began to count," replied Mary ; "and she took from the thick plate. Miss Singleton thought it would be better to mention it before she let her take any more."

" That's Clara Elliot all over !" cried Miss Graves. " These eating fits, as we call them, do come over her now and then. You must limit her at these times to what is sufficient, Miss Halliwell."

" Perhaps she will not be limited," replied Hester.

"Oh yes, she will. You will find her extremely tractable. Control her with gentle authority, as you would a young child, and she will obey you. It is of no use to reason."

And so they found. And they got on

pretty well with Miss Elliot. The worst
days were her laughing ones. She would
suddenly burst into a laugh, no one knew at
what, and nothing could stop her; shrill,
screaming, hearty laughter, one burst upon
another, and she throwing herself backwards
and forwards on her seat with the exertion.
Laughing is contagious, and the first time it
came on the whole school caught it, and fell
into the roar; some went into hysterics, and
others narrowly escaped convulsions. They
had never had such a scene; the teachers
even were affected, and the Misses Halliwell
quite driven out of their self-possession. In
future they led her instantly from the schoolroom, and let her have her laugh out away
from the school-girls. Another annoying
thing was about the pianos. Some one sat
by her whilst she practised, generally Mary
Goring, to whom she had taken a great
fancy; but she would seize a sly opportunity

of bringing both her hands down upon the keys with such force as to break the wires—thump, thump, thump, as one uses a hammer, laughing in delight the whole time. The strength of her hands was astonishing, and they had two pianos damaged in one day. Lucy Halliwell and the teachers declared she used to be worse at the full and change of the moon, but Hester did not see much difference. There was one thing in her favour—that she was perfectly truthful, always telling the straightforward truth fearlessly. No matter whether a fact told against her or for her, out it came, without any softening down. It would seem that the dread of displeasure, which causes other children to equivocate when endeavouring to conceal a fault, was a feeling unknown to Clara Elliot.

On the third day of her residence at Halliwell House, Hester was seated in the drawing-room while Mary Goring took her lesson from the harp-master, when one of the maids announced Mr. William Elliot, and there entered one of the very handsomest young men Hester had ever seen. She did not admire men who are generally called handsome : big, showy, black-curled, prominent-featured, high complexioned, with loud voices, confident manners, and long moustachios. Mr. William Elliot was none of that : tall, he certainly was, and elegant, with features of great beauty, pale and quiet, a sweet look in his hazel eyes, and a pleasant voice and manner that attracted you, whether you would or not. Hester did not know what there was in him to win her heart, but as he held out his hand to her and asked after his sister, it went over to him there and then. Mary continued her playing without notice, for it was the rule of the house that lessons were never interrupted for the entrance of visitors. She had, however, nearly finished.

Clara Elliot came in, giggling and jumping, pulled her brother's face down to kiss, and then flapped herself on the sofa, and began one of those senseless fits of laughing. The harp-master left just then, and Hester was glad of it. Young Mr. Elliot, with a flush on his face, wound his arm about her waist.

"Clara! Clara!" he said, in kind but authoritative tones. "I want to talk to you. Do not laugh just now. Come and look at my new horse."

Her silly laugh subsided instantly. It was evident that her brother had a hold on her affections or her poor mind, and she suffered him to take her to the window. A groom, well mounted, was leading his young master's horse before the house.

"Oh, he is superb!" cried Clara, jumping again as soon as she saw the horse. "When did you buy him, William?"

"Only yesterday."

" Come and look," she uttered, darting across the room, and pulling forward Mary Goring, who was putting the music straight preparatory to leaving the drawing-room; "it's my brother's new horse. Do you know who she is?" she added, as soon as they reached the window—" she is my new sister. Her name's Mary."

He bowed slightly at this unceremonious introduction. Mary would have released herself, but the girl clasped her tightly with her strong hands.

A foolish fancy came over Hester, and perhaps it is foolish to relate it, but that can do neither harm nor good now. As they stood there side by side, William Elliot and Mary Goring, their profiles were turned towards Hester, and she was struck with a singular likeness between the two—the same beautiful cast of features, the drooping eyelid, the arched nostril, and the same sweet look in the mouth.   It struck a chill on her heart. She hardly knew whether it was a presentiment or whether it was the breeze from the door, but the likeness and the chill were both there. She drove it away and forgot it : though she had too good cause to remember it afterwards : and she unwound Miss Elliot's arms and dismissed Mary.

"I hope Lady Elliot's cold is better," Hester said to her visitor.

"Thank you, yes. She talks of driving down to-morrow.   I am glad you are happy, Clara," continued Mr. William Elliot, fondly stroking his sister's hair. "Do you think," he said in a low tone to Hester, as Clara flew off to another part of the room, on some flighty errand, "that the change here promises to be of service to her ?"

Hester said she could not give an opinion : Clara had been with them too short a time ; and presently Mr. Elliot took leave.

As he left the room, Hester turned to ring
the bell, and in that moment Clara flung the
window wide open, and stretched herself
dangerously out of it. Hester's heart was in
her mouth—as the saying goes—and she
sprang towards Clara, and managed to take
the bell-pull with her.

" My dear," she said, " you must not lean
out in this way ; you might fall and kill yourself. Besides, it is too cold for the window to
be opened to-day. Jack Frost is in the
roads."

" I like Jack Frost," she answered. "And
I never fall out of the window. I hold on."

Hester closed the window, taking Clara's
hand in hers, and again came that silly laugh.
It was at sight of her brother, who was going
out at the gate. He looked up with those
handsome eyes of his, and kissed his hand to
her. The groom cantered up, and William
Elliot prepared to mount.

She was like a young cat! Before Hester
well knew she had drawn away her hand,
before she knew she had left her side, she
had flown downstairs and was out in the
road, dancing round her brother's horse.
The horse began dancing too. Clara only
clapped her hands and danced the faster.

Susan rushed out to the gate, and Hester
rushed down the stairs, the bell-pull dragging
after her, which had somehow hooked itself
on to the pocket-hole of her dress. But Mr.
William Elliot was off his steed, quietly; but
quick as a flash of lightning, had thrown the
bridle to the groom, and had his arm round
Clara, leading her in again. Hester met
them at the hall door.

"You must not think me wanting in care,"
she panted to him, the fright having run
away with her breath; "I was not prepared
for her sudden movements. I shall be so
in future."

"Her movements sometimes are sudden," he replied, "but she never comes to harm. There is a providence over her, Miss Halliwell, as there is over a child."

The next day, a very fine one, though cold, Miss Graves came down in the carriage. Lady Elliot's cold was worse, so she had sent her instead, to take Clara for an airing. Clara pouted, and would not go. Miss Graves was at a nonplus.

"Lady Elliot will blame me, and say it was my fault," she said. "She made a point of her going out this bright day. Clara, dear, we shall see such fine things as we go along; we shall see Punch and Judy It is in full work, fife and drum and all, lower down the road."

Punch and Judy was a sight that poor Clara was wild after; there was nothing she enjoyed so much in life. Miss Graves really had passed the show on her way.

This was a great temptation to Clara, and she seemed irresolute, but finally shook her head; she wanted to stay with Mary Goring. Miss Graves then suggested that Mary should accompany them and see Punch too, and Clara eagerly seized at it.

"So you had a visit from William Elliot yesterday," observed Miss Graves, when they had gone to get ready. "What young lady was it he saw here?"

"He only saw his sister," Hester replied, forgetting, as she spoke, the temporary stay of Mary in the drawing-room. "And two sad frights she gave me."

"Yes, he did," returned Miss Graves. "One of the young ladies, he told me."

"Oh, true, I remember now. It was my niece, Miss Goring."

"Then he is surely smitten with her," was the rejoinder of Miss Graves. "He kept talking about her to me last night, and said she was the sweetest girl he had ever seen."

"Ah, young men are apt to say that of all the pretty girls they meet," was Hester's answer; but somehow she thought of that strange chill again.

CHAPTER VII.

CLARA'S ESCAPADE.

EASTER approached, and Clara Elliot went home on the Wednesday in Passion Week to spend some days. On the Thursday she got Mary Goring into her head, and so teased her mother to send for her, that Lady Elliot grew quite cross. In most cases Clara was as easily swayed as a child, but when she did get hold of a fixed idea and turn obstinate over it, there was no moving her. At the dinner-table she refused to eat. "I don't want any dinner," she sullenly remarked; "I want Mary Goring."

"Who in the world's Mary Goring?" inquired Sir Thomas.

"Oh, one of her schoolfellows," replied Lady Elliot. "She has been dinning the name into me all day."

"Nonsense," responded Sir Thomas. "You are putting on more childishness than you need, Clara. Eat your dinner."

"She is not nonsense," retorted Clara. "She is better than you are here. William knows it."

A flush, quite uncalled for, rose to William Elliot's face. "Clara has talked to me about some young lady whom she seems to have taken a fancy to," he explained. "I suppose it is the same."

"You saw her!" burst forth Clara; "you have seen her twice. You know you did."

"Have I?" answered Mr. William.

Lady Elliot interposed, and, to pacify Clara, promised that she should fetch Mary

Goring on the morrow. But the morrow was Good Friday. They went to church. After service some visitors came in, and the day passed without fetching Mary Goring, neither had they seen Clara Elliot so obstinately sullen. Alas! the next morning Clara was missing. The house was searched, but she was nowhere to be found. They supposed she must have risen early, dressed herself, and then must have gone out, unseen by Miss Graves and the servants. Her ͵bonnet, velvet mantle and suite of furs were gone. A strange commotion the house was in. Never had Clara Elliot attempted such an escapade before. Lady Elliot was nearly out of her senses.

"She must have gone after that young girl she was worrying over," cried Sir Thomas, when informed of the disaster. "Mary—what was it? Her schoolfellow."

Nothing more likely. And William Elliot,

the most active of the party, flew downstairs
and into a cab.

The Miss Halliwells were seated at breakfast in the dining-room, when one of the servants entered, and said that Mr. William Elliot
had called and wished to see her mistress.

" Mr. William Elliot at this hour!" repeated Hester, rising from her chair. " Can
anything unpleasant have happened ?"

" You'll never go to him that figure, aunt !"
cried Mary Goring in alarm.

Hester considered, and believed that she
did look singular. For on this Saturday
morning, as many of the pupils had gone
home, the maids were going to turn out part
of the house, and Hester was going to help
them. She had put on a large, old-fashioned
muslin cap, with a spreading border, to save
her head from dust, and a short, buff cotton
bedgown—if the modern reader knows what
that old-fashioned article means.

"He will think Aunt Hester's showing off in her night-cap and night-dress," said Master Alfred Goring, who had gone to them for a three days' holiday. Matthew, the eldest son, had received an appointment in India, and had not long sailed.

"The gentleman is waiting outside," interposed Ann. "He would not go upstairs."

"Dear me! Outside! Never mind my dress, children. I beg your pardon for keeping you there," said Hester, as he entered; "I had no conception that you had not gone into the drawing-room. The truth is, I was a little averse to appearing before you in this attire, but I am going to be busy with the maids. My nephew suggested that you might think it my night-dress, but I can assure you it is not, though I beg you to excuse it."

"It is I who need excuse for disturbing you at this hour," he answered, with a smile, running his eyes over her shoulders and head. And then he told his errand. But they had seen nothing of Miss Elliot, and he hurried away to prosecute the search.

About middle day Lady Elliot arrived, nearly frantic. "A girl like Clara, who wants proper sense to take care of herself!" she uttered. "Suppose she falls into bad hands! Oh, Miss Halliwell, this horrible suspense will kill me."

They could give little consolation to Lady Elliot, and she soon left. In her state of mind she could not remain long in one place. Halliwell House was like a fair that day, and the cleaning got on very badly. Hester soon found she had to leave it to the servants, change her costume, and have a fire lighted in the drawing-room : Mr. Elliot coming, as has been mentioned, in the morning ; Alfred running in and out, looking for her up and down the road, and calling in at the police-station; then Miss Graves coming; then Lady Elliot; then another flying visit from Mr. William; and in the afternoon they were honoured by a visit from Sir Thomas. The family, that day, passed their time running between their own house and Hester's, so certain did they make of the latter's being the point of Clara's journey. Sir Thomas was handsome still, but his manners had grown reserved, and his speech chary; widely different from what had been the impudent and attractive Tom Elliot.

"You perceive, madam," he observed to Hester, "we can only arrive at the conclusion that my daughter must have left home to come in search of Miss—Miss—excuse me, I forget the name."

"Miss Goring."

"Miss Goring. I beg your pardon. May I be permitted to see Miss Goring? Though possibly she may not be able to throw any light on my daughter's movements."

What light was Mary likely to throw, thought Hester. However, there could be no objection to Sir Thomas Elliot's seeing her if he wished. So Mary was called.

An expression of surprise arose to Sir Thomas's face when she answered the summons. He had probably only expected to behold a silly school-girl, and in walked Mary, with her lady-like manners, her handsome half-mourning dress, and her winning beauty. His manner to Hester had been a little patronizing—or she fancied so—but he rose up to Miss Goring the finished gentleman.

" My daughter speaks of you as her friend," he said ; " she was doubtless coming in search of you ; can you offer any suggestion as to where she may have strayed ?"

" No," answered Mary. " Unless "--she

hesitated, while a damask colour flew to her cheek, for it was not pleasant to speak to a father of his daughter's delinquencies— "unless she should have met the show she is so fond of, and have followed it."

"You allude to Punch. But I think it was too early for the ridiculous exhibition to be abroad," replied Sir Thomas, who was aware of his daughter's predilection for the popular amusement.

"Have you suggested it to the police who are in search?" asked Hester. "If she did happen to see it, she would be certain to stray away in its wake."

"No," he said; "it did not occur to me. But I will lose no time in doing so now. I really thank you very much, madam, for the thought." So Sir Thomas Elliot bowed himself out, and they saw him get into his brougham.

The next arrival was Miss Graves again,

just as they were going to tea, which Hester then caused to be carried into the drawing-room. Lady Elliot had sent her.

" This is really dreadful," she exclaimed, taking the cup Hester handed her ; " Lady Elliot is quite beside herself with excitement, picturing all sorts of shocking things happening to the child. And she says it's my fault ; that I ought to have looked better after her. I am quite exhausted."

" I know what I should do," said Lucy. " I should set the bellman to work."

" There is no bellman in London," laughed Master Alfred—the affair was fun to him. " *I* should engage all the Punch and Judies going, and set 'em up at the street corners. She'd be sure to appear before one of them."

" I do not fear her coming back safely," cried Miss Graves. " Who would harm a poor half-witted child like Clara Elliot ?"

Lucy Halliwell looked grave. "How are they to know she is half-witted? And we do hear frightful stories of the wickedness of London."

"Which are all true," eagerly interrupted Alfred. "If they can catch hold of an unprotected female, they cut off her hair and draw her teeth, and the fashionable barbers and dentists give them no end of money for the spoil."

"Be quiet, Alfred."

"It's true, Aunt Lucy. If you don't believe me, you just go into one of the thieves' streets some day, and see how they'd serve you. My! if Miss Elliot has strayed there! won't she come back with a bald head and empty mouth!"

All this was, of course, nothing but nonsense on Alfred's part. He little thought— but it will be better to go on regularly. They were still at tea when Mr. William

Elliot came in again, so pale and fagged that Hester was grieved to see him, and said so.

"I own I am disheartened," he replied. "If Clara is not found before night, I tremble for the consequences to my mother. And where to search, or what to do, more than we are already doing, I do not know."

"I say, here's a visit," exclaimed Alfred, who was then at the window. "Does Miss Elliot wear a white petticoat?"

"What do you mean?" Hester sharply said. For she did not like to hear him joking about it in the presence of William Elliot.

"I am not joking, Aunt Hester," was the boy's answer. "It's a visit at your gate. A carriage without sides, laden with human live stock, and drawn by a Jerusalem pony. What will you bet one of them is not Miss Elliot?"

They all flocked to the window. " Good heavens above !" exclaimed Miss Graves. It *was* Miss Elliot. But in such a trim ! They will never forget the sight.

The vehicle was drawn up before the gate —one of those wide boards on wheels, where you may have seen vegetables and shell-fish hawked for sale. Flat upon it sat a man, who drove the donkey, a woman holding a child, and between them a female figure in a broken straw bonnet, a ragged cotton shawl of no colour but dirt, and a white petticoat. The figure was Clara Elliot ; when she came upstairs they recognised her, not before, and William Elliot's lips turned as white as ashes.

What an object the unfortunate girl pre-sented ! She was not precisely *en chemise* (as the French governess at Halliwell House was wont reproachfully to say to the little girls when she would pounce into their chamber at night and catch them at puss-in-the-corner), but she was not far removed from it. No velvet bonnet and mantle, no furs, no silk dress, and no gloves. No boots, even. Nothing but the disgraceful bonnet and shawl, over the white petticoat, her own stockings, and a pair of slip-shod slippers, which could have no parallel, unless it was in the Crimea, as mentioned by Ensign Pepper. Clara seemed to enjoy the affair amazingly, and threw herself on a chair with bursts of laughter, hugging the shawl round her. Her hair and teeth were safe.

"Does this here young lady belong to here?" began the man, a tall fellow, all skin and bone, with a deformed foot.

They all answered in a breath that the young lady did belong to them, but Mr. Elliot's voice rose highest, demanding to know where she had been detained, and what brought her home in that state.

"I was away on my rounds, gentlefolks," returned the man; "and knowed nothing on it till I come home this a'ternoon, and found the young miss along of my missis. They can tell you about it better nor I can."

The man pushed his wife forward as he concluded. She had mild blue eyes and a hectic colour. And, now that the first shock of their appearance was wearing off, Hester began to like the people. Rough and dark as the man was, common and low as they were in station, she felt sure they were honest and kindly.

"We keep a bit of a shed for coal, ma'am, near to Covent Garden, and for greens and things that my husband can't sell on his rounds," the woman began, addressing herself to Hester, whom she probably took for Clara's mother; "and this morning, about eleven o'clock, as I was coming in from delivering a quarter of a hundred of coals to a customer, somebody lays hold on me and asks if that was the way to Halliwell House, ———— Road." So I said, no, it wasn't, nor anywhere near it; and then I noticed what a odd-looking young person it was, and she burst out laughing (perhaps because she saw me a-staring at her), and up and told me she had been robbed of her clothes. Well, I did not pay no attention to her, for we have all sorts of girls in our part, saving your presence, ladies, but she followed me into our shed, and began playing with my children, and asked me to get a cab and take her home. I asked her if she'd got some money, and she said no, they had taken her purse; but her friends would pay. So after that I put some questions to her, and began to believe her tale, especially as I saw that her underclothes, which they had not touched, was fine, like a lady's."

"Who took your clothes from you, Clara?" interposed Mr. William, in the kind but authoritative tone he sometimes used to her.

"I was coming here to fetch Mary," she answered. "I had walked a good way, and was looking for the turning, but I could not find the right one. Then a woman asked what I wanted, and I told her, and she said she would show me, and took me along with her."

"Well? Go on, Clara," said her brother.

"She took me into a room, up some dirty stairs, where there was another woman. I was angry, and said that was not Halliwell House, and she said we were only going to have some breakfast first. She said that," added Clara, her eyes brightening up, "because I told her I had cheated mamma and all of them, and run away without any. Then she and the other woman took my own things off me, and my pocket, and put these on, and when I cried, they promised I should have them all back again when I got home, and they gave me some bread and bacon."

" What did they do after that ?"

"After that the other woman came out with me, and said she was going to bring me here, but suddenly she was gone, and I could not find her. It was a nasty dirty street, and I did not know my way, so I asked *her*," pointing to the woman in the room.

"It is the same tale she told to me, ma'am," resumed the woman to Hester. "There are wretches in this wicked town that do prowl about to pick up children, and others who can't defend themselves, and rob them of their things. So I believed as the young lady had told the truth, and I kep' her in our back room, along of my young ones, and wouldn't let her go into the street, as she wanted, for she don't seem to be one as ought to be abroad by herself; and I give her a bit of our dinner, such as it was. And when my husband and big boy came home, I persuaded of him to bring her down here, which he didn't want to, and I came along myself; for, says I, her friends will be more satisfied like if I goes to testify that she has been kep' safe since she come into my hands. I'm ashamed as I'd nothing to lend her to put on, in place of them dirty things," added the woman, with an increase in her hectic colour, and lowering her tone; " but this have been a hard winter with us, and I have been forced to put away all but what I stands up in."

There was genuine good feeling betrayed in the woman's speech, and William Elliot's eyelashes glistened, as he turned to look out into the road. His unfortunate sister! what a display it was for him!

"It warn't as I were unfeeling, or thought of my trouble in bringing the young person down, gentlefolks," gruffly spoke up the husband, "nor it warn't as I knew the animal was done up ; but there ain't a busier day throughout the year for us costermongers than Easter Saturday, and I was going out again with a fresh stock, which now I have lost the sale on. Our boy Bill, too, as we've left in charge of the shed and the young ones, can't sell as his mother can."

"You shall be no loser by what you have done, my good man," interposed Mr. Elliot warmly.

"Well, sir, it were my missis as talked me into it, so I won't say as it weren't. 'Suppose it were our own girl, Bill, as were lost,' says she to me, 'shouldn't we be in a peck o' grief over it ? and ain't this one's folks the same ? and ain't it our duty to take her home without delaying of it, and let 'em see that no great harm have come to her?' So, with that, I harnessed in the donkey again, for I had took him out for a rest, and folded a sack for the young person to sit upon, and brought her down."

What more he would have said, if anything, was interrupted by Clara Elliot. She sprang to the tea-table, seized upon a slice of bread-and-butter, which was lying there on a plate, and offered it to the woman. "Take it," she said; "you gave me some of your potatoes to-day."

"Not for me, miss," was the answer; "I can do without it. If I might give it to my little boy instead"—looking at Hester—"I should be glad." She had held the boy in her arms the whole time, but with difficulty, for he seemed to be a most restless child about two years old. "He's always up at the sight of food, ma'am, for he don't get enough of it, and children has such appetites."

William Elliot took the bread-and-butter from Clara, doubled it, and gave it himself to the child. "He shall get enough in future," he whispered to the mother, with one of his kindly looks.

The people went out, William Elliot with them; Alfred followed, and the party upstairs gathered round the window to see them drive away again. The man sat down first, helped up his wife, civilly enough, and they stuck the boy between them on Clara's sack. William Elliot stood by, writing down in his pocket-book the man's address, and Alfred Goring stood at the gate, in a frenzy of delight at the scene. Almost at the same moment Lady Elliot drove up in a hired cab: her own horses were tired.

She came upstairs, and was painfully agitated when she heard the details, although thankful to receive Clara safe and sound. The girl's half-clad, ludicrous appearance, the wretched substitute for her own clothes, the description of her conveyance home, the nondescript vehicle on which she sat in state, on the coal-sack, behind the donkey, the rough costermonger and his half-starved wife, and, worst of all, the girl's utter indifference to the shame!   Indifference! she *enjoyed* the remembrance of the novel ride.   All this was as wormwood to Lady Elliot.

Clara turned restive about going home, and said she would stop where she was, with Mary Goring.   It was thought advisable to give in to her, at any rate for a day or two: and she went dancing upstairs to have her clothes changed, the desirable articles she had been rejoicing over being immediately consigned to the dust-bin.

"Oh, William, what a disgrace!" murmured Lady Elliot to her son, as the red flush came into her pale cheeks, the light into her glistening eye; "better I had no.

daughter, you no sister, than to have her thus ; better that it would please God to remove her from us !"

Little less agitated was he, as he bent before his mother, little less flushed his own face, but it was with pain at hearing such words from her. " Dear mother," he whispered, as he took her hands, "look not upon it in this spirit. Rather be thankful that the affliction is so much lighter than it might be—and especially thankful this day, as I am, that she is restored to us un- harmed."

She strained his hands in hers, before parting with them, and gazed tenderly into his handsome face, feeling thankful for the blessing bestowed upon her in *him*. And, indeed, she had cause to do so : for there are few sons in these degenerate days like William Elliot.

CHAPTER VIII.

SIR THOMAS AND LADY ELLIOT.

So that morning chill, as Hester Halliwell
called it, had worked itself out, and the
tribulation had come. *Was* it her fault?
She asked herself the question every hour
of her life. Perhaps when Lady Elliot
invited Mary to spend some time in her
luxurious home, Hester ought to have
refused. But Lady Elliot pressed for her,
saying what a comfort she would be to their
unfortunate daughter, and Hester was laughed
at for hinting at an objection. Lucy laughed
at her; Miss Graves laughed at her; Frances

Goring, though she was little more than a
child, laughed at her; and when they inquired her grounds, she had none to give,
for not even to herself did she, or could
she, define them. "They live in style, they
keep gay company, servants, carriages; it
will be giving Mary ideas beyond her sphere
of life," were all the arguments Hester could
urge; none difficult to overrule. So Mary
went for a few days at Easter, which would
have been nothing, for she came back perfectly heart-whole : but she went again at
Midsummer to accompany Lady Elliot and
Clara to the seaside, and then the mischief
was done. What else could have been expected, thrown, as she was, into the fascinating society of William Elliot?

But who was to know that he would make
one of the party? No one. In the first
week of Lady Elliot's arrival at Spa (as
good a name as any other for their marine

residence, as it is not convenient to give the right one) she was surprised at being followed thither by her son. He had come for some sea-bathing, he said, and forthwith engaged apartments at an hotel. Nine weeks Lady Elliot remained, and the whole of that time he and Mary Goring were thrown together. Sir Thomas Elliot wrote once, a curt, decisive letter of three lines, demanding how much more time he meant to waste, and Mr. William wrote back that he was studying where he was, just as hard as he could in his chambers. So he was: studying the sweet face and pure mind of Mary Goring. Had Sir Thomas suspected that, his letter might have been more decisive.

"I guessed how it was," Miss Graves said afterwards to Hester. "There were climbings up the cliffs, and ramblings on the beach after sea shells, and readings in the afternoon, and moonlight lingerings in the garden in the evening : Mr. William could not quite deceive me.   I was left to take care of Clara Elliot, while he talked sentiment with Miss Goring."

" Strolling on the beach together, and talking sentiment by moonlight !" uttered Hester, in dismay.   " And you could see all this going on and never write to me !"

" It's the moonlight does it all," peevishly retorted Miss Graves ; "sentimental strolls would come to nothing without it.   The moon puts more nonsense into young heads than all the novels that ever were written.   I'll give you an example.   One night they were all out in the garden, Mr. William, Clara, and Miss Goring.   A long, narrow strip of ground it was at the back of the house, stretching down nearly to the sea.   Tea came in, and Lady Elliot called to them from the window, but no one answered, so I had to hunt them up.   I tied my handkerchief over my head,

for I had a touch of the toothache, and away
I went.   It was an intensely hot night, with
the moon as bright as silver ; and I looked
here, and I looked there, till I reached the
end of the garden.   On the bench there, fast
asleep, with her head resting on the hard
rock behind her, was Clara, and close by
stood William Elliot, with his arm round
Mary, both of them gazing at the moon.
Now, I ask you, Miss Halliwell, or any other
impartial person, whether such a scene could
have been presented to me in broad day-
light ? People are reserved enough then,
and take care to stand at a respectful dis-
tance from each other.   The moon is alone
to blame, and I'll maintain it."

She vexed Hester uncommonly with her
rubbish about the moon.   "As if," thought
Hester, " when she saw them growing fond of
each other, she could not have despatched a
hint of it by the post !"   "What could Lady

Elliot have been thinking of?" she asked
aloud.

"Bless you, *she* saw nothing of it,"
returned Miss Graves. "Her idea was that
William haunted us for the sake of taking
care of Clara, and she was rarely out with us
herself. She makes so much of Mr. William:
it would never enter her imagination that he
could fall in love with anything less than a
lord's daughter. She would see no more
danger in Mary Goring than in me. But
there's no great harm done, Miss Halliwell.
When I was Mary Goring's age I had lots
of attachments, one after the other, and
they never came to anything. A dozen at
least."

Hester thought it very stupid, comparing
herself with Mary Goring. Not that she
wished to underrate Miss Graves, who was
estimable in her way, but she and Mary
were so differently constituted. Miss Graves

full of practical sobriety, without a grain of romance in her composition, all head; while Mary was made up of imaginative sentiment and refined feeling, all heart. The one *would* be likely to have a dozen "attachments" and forget them as soon as they were over; but the other, if she once loved, would retain the traces for all her future life. It was of no use, however, saying so to Miss Graves—she would not have understood it; and Hester was too vexed to argue. Besides, it would not undo what had been done.

Hester had seen it as soon as Mary returned from Spa. There was a change about the girl; a serene look of inward happiness, an absence of mind to what was going on around her, a giving way to dreamy listlessness of thought. And when, in the course of conversation, it came out that William Elliot had made one of the party at Spa, her aunt's surprised exclamation caused the flush in Mary's cheeks to deepen into glowing, conscious crimson. In one of her letters Mary had mentioned William's name, but Hester never supposed he was there for more than a day or two—had taken a run down to see his mother and sister. That suspicious crimson convinced her at once. She wished it anywhere but in Mary's face ; and when Miss Graves went to Halliwell House, a few days subsequently, to spend an evening, Hester spoke to her. Hence the above conversation.

"You need not annoy yourselves over it," persisted Miss Graves, who was anxious to excuse herself. "If they did fall in love with each other—which I dare say they did, and I won't tell any story about it—they will soon forget it, now they don't meet. If you keep her out of sight when Mr. William calls here, he will soon cease coming, and the affair will die a natural death."

"Of course Mary will not be permitted to

see him," rejoined Hester warmly : " but as to the affair dying out, that's another thing."

The crosses that good resolutions meet with ; the ruses young people are up to, unsuspected by old ones! While Hester and Miss Graves were cleverly laying down plans for the separation of the two parties in question, they were actually together in the dining-room below. Upon Hester's descending to that apartment some time afterwards, there she came upon them. They were standing at the open window, enjoying each other's society in the dangerous twilight hour of that summer's night ; in the sweet scent of the closing flowers ; in the calm rays of the early stars—all dangerous together for two young hearts. The saying of " knocking one down with a feather" could not precisely apply to Hester, for you might have knocked her down with half one.

"Well, I'm sure!" uttered Hester, not in her usual tone of polite courtesy. "I did not know *you* were here, sir. Have you been here long?"

"Not long," replied William Elliot, advancing to shake hands.

Not long! It came into Hester's mind, as she spoke, that she had heard the knock of a visitor a full hour before.

She had not seen him for three months, and his good looks, his winning manners, struck upon her more forcibly than ever. Not so pleasantly as they used to do, for the annoying reflection suggested itself—If they won over to him her old heart, what must they have done by Mary's? Hester took her resolution: it was to speak openly to him: and she sent Mary upstairs to Lucy and Miss Graves.

"Mr. Elliot," she began, in heat, "was this well done?"

He looked fearlessly at her, with his truthful eye and open countenance. "Is what well done?" he rejoined.

"I am deeply grieved at having suffered my niece to accompany your mother to the seaside," continued Hester. "Had I known you were to be of the party, she should certainly not have gone."

"Why not, Miss Halliwell?"

"Why not! I hear of ramblings on the sands, and moonlight interviews in the garden —you with Mary Goring. Was this well done, sir?"

"It was not ill done," was his reply.

"Mr. Elliot," Hester went on, "I am a plain-speaking old body, but I have had some experience in life, and I find that plain speaking answers best in the end. You must be aware that such conduct as you have pursued cannot well fail to gain the affections of an inexperienced girl : and my belief is

that you have been wilfully setting yourself
out to win those of Miss Goring."

"I will not deny it: I have tried to win them.
Because, dear Miss Halliwell," he added,
speaking with emotion, "because she first
gained mine.   I love Miss Goring, truly,
fervently, with a love that will end only with
my life.   From the first day I saw her here,
when poor Clara said she had found a new
sister—you may remember it—she never
ceased to haunt me ; her face and its sweet
expression, her manners, her gentle voice,
were in my mind continually, and I knew
they could only belong to a good, pure, and
refined nature.   It did not take long companionship, when we were thrown together,
to perfect that love ; and, that done, I did set
myself out, as you observe, to win hers, in
exchange.   I trust I have succeeded."

Had Hester raced up to the top of the
Monument, where she had never yet ventured,

the run could not more effectually have taken away her breath than did this bold avowal, which, to her ears, sounded as much like rhapsody as reason. "And what in the name of wonder do you promise yourself by all this, sir?" she asked, when her amazement could find speech. "What end?"

"There is but one end that such an avowal could have in view, Miss Halliwell," he replied. "The end, the hope, that Miss Goring will become my wife."

"Well, you will excuse me, Mr. Elliot," said Hester, after a long stare at him, "but I fear you must be crazed."

He burst into laughter. "Why do you fear that?"

"There is no more probability of your marrying Mary Goring than there is of your marrying that chair, sir. So the best thing you can do is to get her out of your head as speedily as you can."

He did not speak for some moments, and the colour mounted to his brow. "What is your objection to me, Miss Halliwell?"

"I suppose you are playing on my simplicity to ask what my objection is," returned Hester. "It is your family that the objection will come from, not mine. The son of the rich and great Sir Thomas Elliot will never be suffered to wed simple Mary Goring."

"Miss Goring is of gentle blood," he remonstrated.

"I trust she is," said Hester, drawing herself up; "though we, the sisters of her mother, are obliged to keep a school for our living. But your friends will look at position as well as gentle blood. May I ask if Sir Thomas and Lady Elliot know of this?"

"Not yet."

"As I thought, Mr. Elliot. Your romance with my niece must end this night."

" It will not, indeed, Miss Halliwell."

" Sir, it shall. And I must observe that you have acted a cruel part. A young lady's affections are not to be played with like a football. However, you have seen her for the last time."

" Allow me to see her once more," he rejoined.

" Not if I know it, sir."

" But for one instant, in your presence," he pleaded. " Surely that can do no harm, if we are to part."

Something came into Hester's brain just then about George Archer—a vision of her last interview with him in Lord Seaford's park. " Why should she deny these two a final adieu?" she asked herself. So she relented, and called Mary down—and Hester reproached herself afterwards with being exceedingly soft for her pains.

Mary shrank to Hester's side when she

came in, but William Elliot drew her away. " I have been avowing to your aunt how matters stand," he said. " She would persuade me to relinquish you ; she thinks such love as ours can be thrown off at will. So I requested your presence here, Mary, that we might assure her our engagement is of a different nature, that we are bound to each other by ties irrevocable in the spirit, as they shall hereafter be made so in reality."

So that was all Hester got for calling Mary. She had paled, and blushed, and faltered, and now she began to cry and tremble, and William Elliot leaned over her, and reassured her with words of the deepest tenderness. Hester saw nothing but perplexity, before them, and not one wink of sleep did she get that night.

One day the renowned physician, Sir Thomas Elliot, was not himself. In lieu of

the stately imperturbability which charac-
terized the distinguished West End practitioner, his manners betrayed a nervousness,
an absence of mind, never before witnessed
in him. To one lady patient, who consulted
him for dyspepsia, he ordered cod-liver oil
and port-wine; to another, far gone in a con-
sumption, he prescribed leeches, and to live
upon barley-water. He had a large influx of
patients that day, and an unusual number of
calls to make from home. Not until the
dinner-hour did he find his time his own.

He went straight to his wife's room, and
sat down upon a low ottoman, which stood
in its midst. Lady Elliot glanced round at
him, somewhat surprised, for it was not often
her liege knight favoured her with his
presence there in the day. She continued
dressing without comment. Sir Thomas
and Lady Elliot rarely wasted superfluous
words one upon the other.

"Can't you finish for yourself and send her away?" cried Sir Thomas, indicating the attendant by a movement of the head.

More surprised still, but not curious (for Lady Elliot, young and handsome as she was yet, really gave one the idea of possessing no interest in what pertained to this present life—or in the one to follow it, for the matter of that), she dismissed the maid, but did not withdraw herself or her eyes from the glass, as she continued her toilette.

"I did not think, Louisa, you could have been such a fool," was the complimentary opening of Sir Thomas Elliot, in low tones of intense indignation.

Lady Elliot looked at him—as well she might—and a flush rose to her face. She paused, however, before she spoke, coldly and resentfully.

"I proved myself that years ago."

Sir Thomas knew to what she alluded—to

her own hasty and unsanctioned union with himself—and a peevish " Tush !" broke from his lips.

"You have proved yourself a greater one now, Louisa, and you must pardon my plainness in saying so.   If you and I rushed into a headlong marriage it ought to have been the more reason for your not leading William into one."

"William !" echoed Lady Elliot, in a startled voice.   It was, perhaps, the only subject that could arouse her.   She idolized her son.

"You have got into this habit of taking your own course, without consulting or referring to me ; going here, going there— doing this, doing that," proceeded Sir Thomas.   "When you went to Spa for an eternal number of weeks, had you informed me that it was your intention to have William and Miss Goring there also, and

make them companions to each other, I
should have put a stop to it. Anyone but
you might have seen the result."

"Result?" faltered Lady Elliot, with
a sickening foreshadowing of what was
coming.

"Of course," angrily repeated Sir Thomas.
"When a young fellow like William is
thrown for weeks into the society of a girl,
lovely and fascinating as—as—the deuce "—
Sir Thomas, at the moment, could not think
of any more appropriate simile—"only one
result can be looked for. And it has turned
up in his case."

"You mean——"

"That he is over head and ears in love
with her; and has been to me this morning
to ask my sanction to their marriage. I
wish you joy of your daughter-in-law, Lady
Elliot."

Lady Elliot scarcely suppressed a scream.

" It is impossible! it is impossible!" she
reiterated, in agitation. " I never thought
of this."

" Then you must have lived at Spa with
your eyes shut. But I can hardly believe
you. To think that you and Eliza Graves
could be moping and meandering all those
weeks, and not see what was going on
under your very noses! Women are the
greatest —— "

What, Sir Thomas did not say, for he
dropped his voice before bringing the
sentence to a conclusion. " I thought
William was at Spa an unaccountable time,
and wrote him word so," he continued ; " but
I never imagined you had that Miss Goring
there."

" You must have known it," returned
Lady Elliot.

" How should I ? I saw she was staying
here the day or two before you went, but

I thought—if I thought at all about it—that, as a matter of course, she returned home. I say you are always acting for yourself, Lady Elliot, without reference to my feelings —if I have any, which, perhaps, you don't believe.   When, the morning of the day fixed for your departure, I was summoned in haste out of town, you might have delayed it until the following one.   Most wives would. But no, not you!   I came back at night, and found you gone.   How was I to know that you took Miss Goring with you ?"

"It is too preposterous ever really to come to anything," observed Lady Elliot, anxious to find comfort in the opinion. "William, with his personal beauty, his talents, and his prospects, might marry into a duke's family if he chose."

"Exactly.   But he chooses to marry into that of a schoolmistress."

"He must not 'choose,'" persisted Lady

Elliot, growing excited ; "he must be brought to reason."

" Brought to what ?" asked the knight.

" Reason."

" I don't know," was the significant reply. " ' Reason ' did not avail in a similar case with you or with me.   William may prove a chip of the old block."

" It never can be permitted," said Lady Elliot vehemently.   " Marry Mary Goring ! It would be disgracing him for life.   William would never prove so ungrateful."

" Leaving your ladyship the agreeable reflection that you were the chief bringer-about of the disgrace.   Looking at the affair dispassionately, I do not see how it is to be prevented.   William possesses money, independently of us.   Enough to live upon."

" Enough to starve upon," scornfully interrupted Lady Elliot.

" Twice, nearly thrice as much as we

enjoyed for many years of our early lives,"
rejoined Sir Thomas in a subdued voice.
"And to them, who are just now spoony
with fantastic visions, 'Love in a cottage'
may wear the appearance of love in a
paradise."

"Can nothing be done—can *nothing* stop
it?" reiterated Lady Elliot.

"One thing may. I should have put it
in force this morning, but that I certainly
thought you must be a party to this scheme,
after what William let out of the goings-on
at Spa."

"And that thing?" she eagerly asked.

"To forbid it on pain of my curse, as I
believe our parents very nearly did by us.
I do not think William would brave it."

Lady Elliot pressed her hands over her
eyes, as if she would shut out recollection of
the years which had followed her rebellious
marriage. The retrospect was one of dire

anguish ; far worse, in all probability, than had been the reality. Her husband turned to leave the room. She sprang after him, and drew him back.

" Oh, Thomas! anything but that. Never curse our boy, whatever betide. Think of the misery our disobedience entailed on us. Do not force *him* into it."

" Then you will let him marry the girl ?"

" Yes, if the only alternative must be our fate over again for him."

" He comes to - night for the answer," continued Sir Thomas, standing with the door in his hand. " What is it to be ? Consent ? I leave the decision to you, for I will not, in this matter, subject myself to after-reproaches."

" Consent," she replied. But Lady Elliot wrung her hands in anger as she said it. She had anticipated so much more brilliant an alliance for her son.

CHAPTER IX.

A FORBIDDEN MARRIAGE.

So sunshine came into Halliwell House, for
William Elliot went there and laid his
proposals for Mary in due form before the
Miss Halliwells. They could not believe
their own ears. He frankly stated that
Sir Thomas and Lady Elliot were not
cordially inclined to the match, for they had
expected him to choose rank and wealth ; but
they had not withheld their consent, and he
was certain Mary would soon win her way
to their entire love. Perhaps this was as
much as Mary Goring could have hoped for ;

indeed more, for in point of worldly great-
ness William Elliot *was* above her.   Hester
suggested that they should not marry till the
" entire love " of Sir Thomas and his wife
had been gained, but Mr. Elliot laughed
at her, and of course Mary thought with
him.   They were both in a maze of enchant-
ment, and common-sense, as Hester understood the word, was out of the question.
Preparations were begun for the marriage,
and for a few weeks the house was the
pleasantest of the pleasant.

" I told you it would turn out well,"
triumphantly exclaimed Miss Graves one
day when she came down to see Clara
Elliot.

" But you told us it would turn out well by
coming to nothing," laughed Lucy.   " You
have been away a whole month, Miss
Graves ; where have you been ?   Clara
said to Birmingham, but the information

she picks up is not always to be depended on, and William did not seem to know."

"I went to Birmingham first, then to Cheltenham, and then back to Birmingham again. You will never guess what for, unless you have heard. Lady Elliot knew."

"We have heard nothing. Lady Elliot does not come here; when she wants to see Clara she sends for her."

"That's to show her pique at William's choice," cried Miss Graves. "I went away for my sister's wedding.'

"Your sister? Mrs. Archer?"

"Yes. It is an excellent thing for her. She was lady-housekeeper, you know, at old Hazzelrigg, the button-maker's; and one morning, quite unexpectedly, he asked her to marry him. She did not know whether to say yes or no, and she sent for me down to Birmingham. I found he was a martyr to

illness, and wanted a wife to nurse him.
'Oh, marry him,' said I to her; 'he's only
a poor old cripple, without much use in his
legs; but you'll get a good home, and be
mistress of it instead of manager.' So she
told him she would, and we two went to
Cheltenham, and took lodgings there, for she
didn't care exactly to have the wedding in
Birmingham, in the face of all his married
daughters and their families. They went to
the house, I believe, and gave it him well,
when they found what he was going to do;
but he would not give in to them, and at the
proper time he had an invalid carriage, and
was brought to Cheltenham, and they were
married. Afterwards he told her how his
daughters had gone on at him, and she said
if she had known that she would not have
had him. We returned to Birmingham at
once, and I stayed a few days with them
before coming back. That's the history;

and instead of being Mrs. Archer she's Mrs. Hazzelrigg."

"I wish her joy," said Lucy heartily. Hester was thinking of her former husband.

"Joy!" echoed Miss Graves; "that's an empty compliment in her case. But he is said to be worth a hundred thousand pounds. It is, however, chiefly settled on his family, and my sister would not wish it otherwise. But now about your wedding here. Lady Elliot will not speak of it, and I could get at nothing. It is to be pretty soon, I find. Where are they to live?"

"Mr. Elliot has taken a pretty house in the Regent's Park," said Hester.

"Bad locality,' cried Miss Graves. "Always damp. What sort of a style do they mean to set up in?"

"A sufficiently sumptuous one, I call it," answered Hester; "though he thinks it very moderate.   I advised them to begin in a small way, more in accordance with his own than his father's income, and he listened to me.   Two maids and a man they will keep ; no carriage ; only William's horse."

"He will be rich when Sir Thomas dies," remarked Miss Graves.

"But he and Lady Elliot may live many years."

"I suppose Mary is busy, getting her things ready."

"Busy all day long," said Lucy.   "Excepting when William is here : and that's every evening.   The half-past five omnibus is sure to bring him."

"Half-past five !" echoed Miss Graves. "What time does he dine, then ?"

"In the middle of the day, I believe.   He has discovered that dining early is good for his constitution, and never feels well, he says, without an early tea. So that he takes with us. We have it up here in the drawing-room every evening, visitor fashion."

" That's his depth," said Miss Graves. "Good for his constitution! Does Mary see through it ?"

" We do," laughed Lucy. "Sometimes he gets Hester to give Mary a lesson in housekeeping, and he sits listening to it with the most serious face imaginable; but you should catch a glimpse of his handsome eyes, dancing with merriment. He is learning about legs of mutton and apple tarts, he will say, and that sends Frances Goring off into fits of laughter almost as bad as poor Clara Elliot's. But I must say, in one respect, Hester is cruel to him."

" How ?"

" She is so tantalizing. She professes to allow them interviews — makes a boast of it, indeed—but before they have had time to say a word to each other, in she goes, and breaks it up. Very exasperating it must be to Mr. William."

" I limit their interviews to three minutes, explained Hester, "and look at my watch that they may not exceed it. My dear mother brought me up in these punctilious manners, and I approve of them."

"What a shame!" cried Miss Graves. "I should take her out for a walk, were I William Elliot, and talk to her then."

" He did try once," said Lucy. "He asked Hester to let Mary go, but she offered herself instead, and he has never asked since. I do think it is too bad; but Hester is the manager, so I can't interfere."

"I think it's a great deal too bad," repeated Miss Graves. "Why, they get no courting at all. It is a contrast to Spa, I can tell you."

"They had too much of it," said Hester. "Mary is occasionally invited, with Clara, to spend the day at Lady Elliot's, and——"

"Is she cordial with Mary again?" interrupted Miss Graves.

"She has had her there lately. I expect at first she made a merit of necessity; but she grows more cordial with every visit, and is almost as fond of her as she used to be before she knew of William's preference."

"That is pleasant," said Miss Graves. "What were you going to say?"

"Why—the carriage brings them home at night," remarked Hester. "Mary and Clara, escorted by Mr. William; and a nice time those two must have of it, for Clara is safe to go to sleep the instant they get in, and never wake till they get out. Plenty of time for talking secrets then, I hope."

"That's capital!" exclaimed Miss Graves,

clapping her hands. "It makes up for your barbarity, Miss Halliwell."

"You may call it capital," returned Hester, "but it is against my old-fashioned notions of propriety. I hinted so to Mr. William. How he laughed! I laughed, too, and could not help it, when he told me I was a good old dragon of a guardian. Then he changed to seriousness, as he took my hand in his, that sweet, earnest expression rising to his face, and whispered that I could not wish to protect Mary more faithfully than he would do, for that she was dearer to him than ever she was to me. Altogether, things go on very nicely," concluded Hester, "and we are very happy."

They were happy. But an end came to it, as it comes for the most part to all things that are joyful and bright in life. And then Hester asked herself how she could ever have been deluded into the belief that the son of Sir Thomas and Lady Elliot would really espouse Mary Goring.

A telegraphic summons came early one morning to the popular physician, Sir Thomas Elliot. He was wanted in all haste at Middlebury. Sir Thomas hastened to the Paddington station, caught the express train, and was with his patient—a lady—in the afternoon. Her medical attendant was Dr. Ashe ; and a Mr. Warburton was also called in. When in conversation, the discourse of the medical men led to matters foreign to their patient— no very rare occurrence in medical consultations.

" I should like to know what her previous constitution has been," remarked Sir Thomas to Dr. Ashe, speaking in reference to the patient. " I presume you have been her usual medical attendant."

" No, I have not," replied Dr. Ashe—who

was only called "Dr." according to the Middlebury fashion ; "this is the first time I have attended her. Dr. Goring used to be the family attendant. But she must have enjoyed pretty good health, for he has been dead—let me see—more than two years, and no one has been called in to her since."

Dr. Goring! Sir Thomas Elliot pricked up his ears, and a flash of intelligence darted into his mind. She who was soon to be his son's wife was a native of Middlebury, and the daughter of a medical man. This Dr. Goring, then, must have been her father. He would ask a few particulars.

"What sort of a man was Dr. Goring?" he suddenly said. "Respectable? Popular?"

"Very much so," was the reply of Dr. Ashe.

"Until that nasty business occurred about his wife," broke in Mr. Warburton. "He lost both respect and popularity then."

"What business was that?" inquired Sir Thomas.

"She was recovering from an illness—one of the nicest little women you ever saw—in fact, she was all but well," observed Dr. Ashe. "I had seen her in the morning—for I attended her with all her children—and told her that the next day she might move into the drawing-room. That was about eleven o'clock. By five in the afternoon she was dead."

"What from?" was the question of the physician.

"Poison, Sir Thomas."

"Poison!" echoed Sir Thomas Elliot.

"Strychnia."

"By whom administered?"

"There was the question," said Dr. Ashe. "It never has been cleared up from that day to this. With some people poor Goring got the credit of it; but I believe the man to have been as innocent as I was. Nay, I am sure of it."

Sir Thomas Elliot rose from his chair in a perturbed manner. His son about to marry the daughter of a man suspected of——! He sat down again.

" The case was published in the *Lancet*," resumed Dr. Ashe ; " of course, without casting any conjectures as to the administerer."

" I remember now—I remember reading it," cried Sir Thomas. " But it never struck me that—— What were the grounds for suspecting the husband ?"

" In my opinion, I say, there were no grounds," repeated Dr. Ashe. " A few only may have thought so, in just the first blush of the affair. I never saw a more affectionate husband than Goring was ; and he had nothing to gain by her death—everything to lose."

" The insurance money," suggested Mr. Warburton.

" Nonsense! I know some cast it in his teeth—very unjustly, if they had only considered the facts. Mrs. Goring had a clear income of three hundred a year—an annuity which died with her: did not go to her husband or children, understand, Sir Thomas—absolutely died with her. She had insured her own life some years before for three thousand pounds for the benefit of her children. But what is a sum of three thousand pounds in comparison with three hundred a year? And Goring did not touch the money; he invested it for the children. He was a maligned man."

" Was he accused of the crime?" asked Sir Thomas.

" Oh no—no; nothing of that sort. At his wife's interment—I never saw such a crowd in the churchyard before—some voices

hissed him; 'Murderer!' 'Poisoner!' that
was the extent. But if ever grief was genuine
in this world, it was Goring's for the loss of
his wife. They were on the wrong scent,"
muttered Dr. Ashe in a lower tone.

"Dr. Goring, unfortunately, did not show
out quite clear upon another point," interrupted Mr. Warburton. "There was a
governess residing with them, a Miss
Howard, and he was too attentive to her;
but Goring was a free man at all times in his
manners with women. Some said it was her
fault; that she laid herself out to attract
him; and altogether the affair had given
pain and annoyance to Mrs. Goring. So
Miss Howard received warning to leave, and
the little Gorings were to be sent to school.
Before the change was made, Mrs. Goring
was poisoned!"

"Was this governess suspected?" inquired
Sir Thomas Elliot.

" I don't know what other people may have done," interposed Dr. Ashe warmly. " I had my opinion upon the point, and always shall have. But it does not do to speak out one's opinions too freely. There was no proof."

" Where was the strychnia procured ?"

" From Goring's own surgery. At least, such was the conclusion drawn, for he kept some there ; though whether the bottle had been touched, or not, he could not himself tell. Mrs. Goring had dined, and was asleep on her bed, the nurse having gone to her dinner. During her absence, the poison was introduced into a glass of water, which, as was customary, stood at the bedside, and Mrs. Goring, when she awoke, drank of it. Goring was in the garden the whole of this time—never came into the house at all, as the servants testified, until aroused by the screams in Mrs. Goring's room. Miss

Howard was in the dining-room, which adjoined the surgery, and the servants equally testified that if she had quitted it to go upstairs they must have heard her. So the case was wrapped in mystery, and remains so."

"The worst feature was Mr. Goring's marrying the woman afterwards," observed Mr. Warburton.

"Marrying *her!*—the governess!" exclaimed Sir Thomas Elliot.

"He did. She was dismissed from the house on Mrs. Goring's death ; but twelve months afterwards Miss Howard became Mrs. Goring."

"Why, the man must have been mad !' uttered Sir Thomas.

"He was wrong there," said Dr. Ashe. "I told him so. But what I said went for nothing, for he was bent on it. His death was a mystery also : I could never fathom it.

He married this girl, Sir Thomas, went off
with her for a fortnight, and came back so
changed that we hardly knew him. He
started on the journey a gay, healthy man ;
he returned wasted in frame, broken in
spirits, and in two months was laid in his
first wife's grave. There was no particular
complaint, but he wasted away to death—
literally *pined* away, it seemed."

"And pined in silence," added Mr. Warburton ; "for he would never acknowledge
himself ill."

"I see, gentlemen," returned Sir Thomas ;
"it was a bad affair altogether, from beginning to end ; one not too well calculated to
bear the light of day."

"At any rate, the light of day has
never been thrown upon it," answered Dr.
Ashe.

"And the daughter of such a man shall
never become William's wife," mentally con-

cluded Sir Thomas Elliot.   " But, to go back to the next room, gentlemen," he added aloud.   " My opinion——"

We need not follow their consultation for their patient.   It came to an end, and Sir Thomas Elliot went steaming up to town again by the first train.

CHAPTER X.

MOTHER AND SON.

THE train by which Sir Thomas Elliot went up to London happened to be a slow one, stopping at every station, which drove the physician into a fever nearly as great as that of the poor lady he had been to visit, he was so intensely eager to meet his wife —a compliment he had not paid her of recent years.

Lady Elliot seized with avidity upon the information. It was a pretext for *demanding* of William to break off the match. "Of course," she said, "he will not think of entering upon the connection now."

A presentiment struck Hester that something was wrong when Ann went into the schoolroom and said Sir Thomas Elliot wanted her. These presentiments do come across us sometimes, without our knowing why or wherefore. Do they ever fail of being borne out? They never did with Hester. Surely there was nothing unusual, nothing to create surprise or uneasiness, in Sir Thomas Elliot's paying a morning visit to the Miss Halliwells, connected as the families were about to be; yet, before Hester reached the drawing-room door, all that was to take place seemed to flash upon her. Sir Thomas turned at her entrance, and prefaced what he had to say by stating that he had been called to Middlebury the previous day on professional business.

"I am aware of it," answered Hester. "Mr. William took tea with us last evening, and mentioned that you were gone there."

"How did he know it?" growled Sir Thomas under his breath. "Called in and heard it from his mother, I suppose. Well, madam, to be brief — for I have patients waiting for me now at home, and knew not how to spare time for coming here—I am concerned to tell you that I received an account of the late Dr. Goring ('Doctor,' as I hear him universally called, though I find he was only a general practitioner) which has considerably surprised me."

"In what way, sir?" asked Hester, with outward calmness, though her heart was fluttering sadly.

"Why, madam, can you be ignorant that —you must pardon my speaking plainly; I only repeat the statement as it was given to me—that Dr. Goring was suspected of having poisoned his wife?"

"Oh, sir!" interrupted Hester, "do not, I beseech you, speak so injuriously of the dead. Dr. Goring was an honourable man, of a kind, good nature, a gentleman and a scholar, one not capable of so dreadful a crime. I am cognisant of all the particulars, and I assert that whoever accused Dr. Goring of killing her was guilty of a wicked calumny."

"But he *was* suspected?" urged Sir Thomas.

"Not by those who knew him, and knew the circumstances."

"There was someone else mixed up in the affair—a governess."

"Unhappily there was," answered Hester. "Say, rather, the author of it all, Sir Thomas," she added, with emphasis. "But I must only say this in a whisper, and to you."

"Who afterwards became Dr. Goring's

wife," continued Sir Thomas, looking stead-fastly at Hester.

" I am ashamed to say she did."

" Well, madam, this is just what I have heard. We will not differ about minor details; the facts are the same. Under the circumstances, you cannot wonder that I have forbidden my son to think more of Miss Goring."

"Oh, Sir Thomas Elliot!" exclaimed Hester. " It will be a cruel thing!"

"I hope not. I do not wish to hurt the young lady's feelings more than is unavoid-able; and I cast no reproach upon *her*. I believe her to be, personally, most estimable. Still, I must have due consideration for my son's honour and for that of his family; and a young lady liable to be pointed at as—as —in short, as the daughter of Dr. Goring of Middlebury, cannot be eligible to become William Elliot's wife."

He said more, but Hester was too grieved, too stunned, to hear clearly what it was. Nothing could soften the bare and abrupt fact that he peremptorily broke off the negotiation for an alliance with Mary Goring. She watched him get into his carriage from the window, her heart painfully failing her. *How* was she to break it to Mary?

That same day, a little later, William Elliot sat with his mother in her morning-room. Marks of agitation were on both countenances; and to little wonder, for she was seconding what her husband had previously said to him, indignantly forbidding his intended marriage, and he listened in a state of rebellion, as indignantly remonstrating. Never, until now, had William Elliot been aroused to anger against his parents; he was not only a dutiful son, but fondly attached to them.

"Why persist in attributing our conduct to caprice, when we are only actuated by a desire for your honour and happiness?" urged Lady Elliot. "There is no help for it, William. You cannot marry one whose father's name was stained with sin."

"I have made it my business to inquire the particulars of the prejudice against Dr. Goring," returned Mr. Elliot. "When my father stated to me, last night, what he had heard at Middlebury, I determined to seek out a fellow I know who comes from there. Stone, his name is ; he is reading for the Bar ; his chambers are next to mine, in Lincoln's Inn. I have been with him this morning, and heard the details of the affair, perhaps more fully than my father did ; and I would stake my life on Dr. Goring's innocence."

"As if a London law-student, young and credulous as yourself, could know anything

of such particulars !" slightingly spoke Lady
Elliot.

" He was at home when it happened,"
retorted William, his pale face flushing with
pain at his mother's tone.   " His father,
Stone, of Middlebury, was solicitor to
Dr. Goring ; they lived within a few
doors of each other ; the families were
on terms of intimacy, and young Stone
knows all, even to the minute details.
Do not cast ridicule upon what I say,
mother.   Dr. Goring was a cruelly aspersed
man."

" No," said her ladyship.

" Yes," persisted Mr. Elliot.   " Were I a
perfectly uninterested party, I should say the
same.   I look at the facts dispassionately,
and my reason tells me so."

" How very obstinate you are, William !
Do you dispute that Mrs. Goring died the
death she did ?"

" No. On that point, unhappily, there is no room to doubt."

" Or that some one residing in the house must have dealt her death out to her ?"

" So it would seem."

" Then who was that person ?"

" Not her husband. There was another."

" The governess. But Dr. Goring afterwards made that woman his second wife. Was there no crime, no dishonour in that, William ?"

William Elliot sat silent, his brow contracting.

" He cannot be defended there; it was an unseemly connection; but Dr. Goring never would, or did, credit anything against her, and his having made her his wife proves that. He was a most honourable-minded, kind man, and a universal favourite. I tell you what, mother—had you and Sir Thomas not been secretly averse to my marriage yourselves, I should never have had Dr. Goring's conduct brought up as a plea against it."

"You are prejudiced and unjust," said Lady Elliot. "If we argue until night, we shall not agree."

"I am sorry for that," observed William; "for, if so, only one course is open to me."

"What is that?" cried Lady Elliot quickly.

"Though I assure you, my dearest mother, it will be with the very utmost reluctance that I adopt it—that of marrying without your consent."

Lady Elliot half sprang from her seat, and a sound of pain, too sharp for a groan, escaped her.

"My happiness, my very life, are bound up in Miss Goring," he resumed. "To separate us now, after allowing the intimacy, sanctioning the measures for our marriage,

would be cruel injustice. I will not submit
to it."

" William," she uttered in visible agitation,
"you cannot marry in defiance of your
father and mother. You dare not."

" Not without deliberation, and in grief and
great repugnance, have I formed the resolution ; but I owe a duty to Miss Goring, as well
as to my father and mother. The proposed
allowance to me I shall not expect or ask
for. The house I have taken I must give
up, and look out for a smaller one ; and we
must make my own income suffice for our
wants, until I can bring my profession into
use."

" You speak of duty to Miss Goring," she
resumed with emotion ; " have you forgotten
that to your parents lies your first and fore-
most duty—a duty ordained of God?"

" Mother, I have forgotten nothing. I
have debated the question with myself upon

all points.   And I believe that I am doing
right in marrying."

" In   defiance," she   repeated, "of   your
father and mother ?   *In defiance ?*"

" I am sorry that they drive me to it."

For several minutes Lady Elliot's agitation had been increasing, and it appeared
now to rise beyond control.   Two crimson
spots shone on her pale cheeks, her slight
frame shook with agitation, and her hands
were cold and moist as she grasped those
of her son.

" Listen, William," she said; " I will tell
you a painful tale.   You may have gathered
something of it in your boyhood, but not
its details.   *Will* you listen ?   Or are you
going to despise even my words ?"

" My dear mother!   You know I will
listen, in all reverence.   If you would but
afford me the opportunity to be reverent
in all things!"

" I was a happy girl at home. My mother died—and then I owed my father a double duty. I was but a child, barely eighteen, when a young man, handsome, William, as you are now, was introduced to us. He was extravagant, random, but he loved me; and that was all I cared for. Our attachment became known to my father. He deemed this gentleman no eligible match for me; he doubted his ability, in many ways, to render me happy; and he put a stop to our meetings. He forbid me to think more of him; he said if I did, in spite of his veto, pursue the acquaintance, that he would discard me from his house for ever. On the other side, the friends were equally averse to it; and *his* parents bid him, though in all kindness, shrink from the fruits of disobedience. His father, a clergyman, implored of him not to brave it; he told him that deliberate disobedience to a parent was surely visited

on a child's head.   Happy for us both had
we attended to their counsel ; but youth, in
its ardour, sees not things as they are.   In
after   years,   when   soberness,   experience,
judgment have come to them, they look back
and marvel at their blindness.   We, he and I
—oh, William ! that I should have such an
avowal to make to you !—set our parents'
interdiction at nought, and I ran away from
my home to become his wife.   That man
was Thomas Elliot, your father."

She was excessively excited.   Her son
would have begged of her not so to disturb
herself, but she waved away his interrup-
tion.

"We gloried in having deceived them.
Not so much for the deceit in itself—we had
not quite descended to that—as that we had
obtained our own will.   But, William, how
did it work ?   How does such sin always
work ?"

She paused, almost as if she waited for an answer. He did not speak.

"Look abroad in society, and watch the results; scan narrowly all those who have thus rebelliously entered on their own career. Sooner or later, more or less bitterly, retribution comes home to them. It may rarely be attributed to its right cause, even by themselves; and many there are who would laugh at what I am now saying. None have had the cause that I have to note these things; and it is from long experience, from repeated and repeated instances I have witnessed of the confirmation of my opinion, that my firm conviction has been formed. Some are visited through poverty; some in their children; some in themselves, in their unhappy life. We, William, have had a taste of all. In the early years of our union it was one struggle to live; perhaps you remember yet our pinchings and contrivances. My children

died off, save you, one after the other; and
she, Clara, who remained to us"—Lady
Elliot sank her voice to a whisper—"were
better off had she followed them. I and he
whom I chose have had no mutual happiness,
for we found that we were as unsuited to
each other as man and wife can be. My
father never forgave me; so, for his remaining years, and they were many, or seemed
so, I was an alien from him. Thus have I
dragged through life, trouble upon trouble
pursuing me, and the consciousness of my
sin ever haunting me. William, before you
talk of marrying Mary Goring, you should
know what it is to brave and live under a
parent's curse."

William Elliot did not reply, but his face
wore a look of keen anxiety.

"At morning, at the sun's rising; at evening, when it sets; in the nervousness of the
dark night; in the glare of mid-day, was my

disobedience present to me ; heavily, heavily it pressed upon me. I would have forfeited all I possessed in life, even my remaining years, to have redeemed it ; and, William, I prayed to God that He would in mercy keep *my* children from committing the like sin."

Lady Elliot paused for breath ; and her face, a sufficiently young face still in years, but not in sorrow, was blanched, and her eyes were strained on her son.

" I prayed it as the greatest mercy that could then be accorded me. I have never ceased praying for it. William, will you, my ever-loving and dutiful boy, be the one to set that prayer at naught ?"

No answer. His lips were white as her own.

" You were my first-born, my first and dearest ; in you rests all the hope left to me ; what other comfort have I in life ? I have said to myself now and then, ' The closing

years of my existence shall be brighter than
the earlier ones, for my darling son shall be
my stay and solace!' Oh, William, William!
give me your promise now! I kneel to beg
it. Say that you will never marry without
our consent."

The lines of his pale face were working ;
it seemed that he would speak, but could not.
Lady Elliot had shrunk down at his feet and
would not rise.

" If you bring upon yourself this same
wretched fate, which has been our bane, I
shall never know another moment's peace.
I shall repine that you did not die in infancy;
I shall wish, more than I have ever done,
that I may die and be at rest from the
trouble and care of this weary world.
William, it is your mother who pleads with
you. Promise that you will never marry in
disobedience."

How could he resist such pleading—he,

with duty and affection implanted in his heart by nature, and hitherto fondly cherished? It was not possible. "Mother, I promise it," he uttered, "as long as you and my father shall live. After that——"

"Nay, I will not extort a further promise. You will then be your own master. But until that time — you pass your word, William?"

"I do. You have it."

"Thank God! Now I am at rest."

"Which is equivalent to undertaking never to marry at all," murmured the unhappy young man, as he rose and quitted the room. "Oh, Mary! how shall I part with you?"

Hester was still standing at her drawing-room window after witnessing the departure of Sir Thomas Elliot, when she saw Lady Elliot's carriage drive to the gate, and Miss Graves alight from it.

"I say," she cried, in her familiar way, as

she entered, " what in the world is up ?   Do
you know what I am sent here for ?"

" Not exactly," replied Hester, though a
dim suspicion floated through her mind.

" To take away Clara."

" To remove her entirely ?"

" Yes ; as far as I understand it.   I was in
the storeroom, having a dispute with the
cook about some pickles — for Lady Elliot
looks to me to see to things ; and if all the
pickles and preserves in the house fermented
and turned to froth and uselessness, she
would never interfere herself to order it
stopped—when one of the servants came in
and said I was wanted in her ladyship's
room.   So up I went. 'Oblige me,' she
said, ' by going to Halliwell House and
bringing home Clara. The carriage is getting
ready. Give my compliments to the Miss
Halliwells, and say they will have the kindness to forward me the account by post and

send up her boxes by the carrier.' Those
were her very words."

Hester made no remark.

"I never was so thunderstruck," continued
Miss Graves. " 'To fetch her home and
her boxes!' I said. 'For good?'

" ' Yes,' answered Lady Elliot.

" ' Have the Miss Halliwells offended your
ladyship?' I asked. 'Have you discovered
any cause of complaint against them?'

" 'Not against the Miss Halliwells,' she
replied in her stiff way.

"Unsociable she is at times, but she was
so much so this morning I did not dare to
say another word. So all I could do was to
put on my bonnet and obey orders; but I
have been wondering the whole of the
way down; and I met Sir Thomas in his
brougham a little higher up. Had he been
here?"

" He has not long left," replied Hester.

"Well now, do, Miss Halliwell, tell me what's amiss.   Is it anything wrong between William and your niece?   Have they quarrelled?"

"They are not likely persons to quarrel," rejoined Hester.   "No; but Sir Thomas wishes to break off the marriage."

"Goodness me!" uttered Miss Graves. "And shall you allow him?"

"How can I help it?"

"Then of course you'll bring an action against them for breach of promise, and all that?"

"Breach of promise!" echoed Hester, with a sickly smile.   "Do not talk so, Miss Graves."

"Well, I should.   What is their plea?"

"You must excuse my entering upon that. It is not," she hastily added, "anything personally connected with Mary.   It relates to family matters; that much I will say."

" Does the objection come from Mr. William ?"

" I think not. I am not sure."

" Well, it is incomprehensible," ejaculated Miss Graves. " I am sorry for Mary. It is a shabby trick to serve her."

Hester winced. " Shall I go and see that Clara is made ready ?" she said.

" She must be made ready. Lady Elliot will not be pleased if I keep her horses waiting too long. By the way," added Miss Graves, " a thought has struck me, and it never did till this moment. Last night, after I went up to bed, I went down again for a book I thought I had left in the drawing-room. It was not there, and I went to the dining-room. I had my hand on the door, when I heard the voices of Sir Thomas and Mr. William ; very fast indeed they were talking ; and I wondered, for Sir Thomas rarely talks much either with his wife or son.

I suppose it had something to do with this business."

Hester supposed so likewise. She withdrew; and soon Miss Graves left the house with Clara Elliot. Nothing was said to the child but that she was going home for the day. Neither did Hester say anything in the house: the burden of her thoughts still was, how should she break the tidings to Mary Goring? She did not go again into the schoolroom, at which Lucy was surprised; but she felt unequal to it. And the evening came, and still she had said nothing.

But the evening brought William Elliot. Hester knew his knock, and ran out of the drawing-room, where they were seated at tea, and called to the servants to show him into the dining-room, not to let him come up; and then she went down herself.

"Oh, William!" she exclaimed, unable to restrain her tears, "what is to be done?"

He took her hands, kind as ever, but his own were unsteady, and his face wore an unnatural paleness.

"What does Mary say? How does she bear it?" were his first words.

"I have not dared to tell her. I did not know how."

"That is well. She had better hear it from me."

"From you! Oh no! She ought not to see you."

"Believe me, yes," he firmly rejoined. "None can soothe it to her in the telling as I can."

"It is the first shock that will be the worst, and I dread it for her."

He turned from Hester, put his arm on the window-frame, and leaned his forehead upon it. She did not like to witness his emotion; his whole attitude bespoke despair.

"Let me see her," he resumed.

Hester reflected, and believed it might be best. For what was she—what were all to her—in comparison with William Elliot? "One promise," she said. "You are not going to talk to Mary of a continued engagement, or—a—private marriage? Excuse me, but I have heard of such things being done."

"No; I give you my honour. I have already given it to my mother. This evening is to close my intercourse with Mary; and the interview I ask for is that we may bid each other farewell. I have no alternative—none. My mother—" he paused, and a sort of shudder seemed to come over him—"my mother pointed out—that is—I would say—she exacted a promise from me that I would never marry clandestinely— without her full consent. And I gave it."

"Quite right," said Hester. "You could not have done otherwise."

"And now that they have taken this prejudice against Mary's family, to ask for consent would be fruitless. So there is no hope, and I cannot help myself. But they had better"—he lowered his voice to a whisper—"have destroyed us both, as her mother was destroyed. It would have been more merciful."

Hester went upstairs to the drawing-room and beckoned Mary out.

"Oh, aunt!" she said, "what is all this? Is anything the matter?"

"Yes, dear child, there is," answered Hester through her tears, as she fondly stroked down her hair. "I have known it all day, and I could not tell you. William Elliot will; he is in the dining-room. Now do not agitate yourself."

"But what is it? Are we"—she trembled excessively—"is he——"

"Go to him, my darling. It is very cruel,

but he will soothe it to you better than I can." So Mary went into the room, and Mr Elliot moved forward and closed the door behind her, while Hester paced the hall outside like a troubled ghost.

William Elliot drew Mary across the room in silence and folded her head down on to his breast and held it there.

" What is the matter?" she asked, scarcely above her breath, while she shook visibly. " My aunt said she did not know how to tell me."

" Neither do I, Mary. Yet, told it must be. Can you bear it—whatever it may be?"

" I will try to. I have borne some cruel things in my life."

" We are to be separated."

She had thought nothing less from the moment she saw her aunt's agitation. She did not speak ; only raised one hand and laid

it on her chest. William Elliot held the
other.

"After to-night we are to be as strangers,"
he added. "And this is to be our last meeting on earth."

"By your own wish?" she murmured.

"Mary!"

The tone of reproof, though it was mixed
with tenderness, caused her tears to come.

"Then who is doing it?"

"My father and mother."

"For what reason?"

William Elliot hesitated. "It is a prejudice they have taken against the memory
of your father; your aunt can explain it. I
will not, for I do not share in it."

"And this interview is to be our last!" she
moaned.

"Mary, I could have married you still, for
I am my own master, and my property is
sufficient to live quietly upon until I get my

profession into play. But it would have been a marriage of defiance; and you, perhaps, would not enter into such."

She shook her head. "No—no."

"And so have brought down anger from on high upon us, for disobedience."

She shivered, and held up her hand for him to desist.

"Such a marriage as was my father and mother's," he continued in a whisper. "She told me so to-day. She says that a curse clung to them for years; always has clung to them; and she implored me not to bring the like upon myself. She knelt to me—Mary, do you hear?—my mother knelt to me!"

"Yes, I hear all. Poor Lady Elliot!"

"Could I refuse to promise obedience not to enter into a rebellious marriage? And my mother also worked upon my duty and affection. Though I know not, in justice to you, whether I ought to have promised."

" There was no other course," she sadly answered. " I would not have married you, William, in opposition to your parents."

"Ah, Mary! they think they have done a fine thing in separating us ; they say they have acted for my welfare and happiness. That people can so delude themselves ! It will cost us dear."

Her tears broke into sobs and he clasped her closer to him, their hearts beating one against the other. Let us leave them to themselves : these sort of partings are too sacred to be touched upon.

It was quite dusk when he came out to leave, and Hester was walking about still. The hall lamp was lighted, and she saw the traces of emotion on both faces. Yes, on both ; and you need not despise William Elliot for that. We do not, many of us, throughout our lives, go through such a trying interview as that had been to him.

" God bless you, dear Miss Halliwell," he said, " and thank you for the many courtesies, the kindness you have shown me. Thank you, also, for your care of Clara : I do not know whether anyone else has thought to do it. I hear she is removed."

" Yes. To-day."

He wrung Hester's hand and turned again to Mary. " And God bless *you*," he added, in a whisper : " remember, Mary, what I have said. Though they have succeeded in separating us, though your path must lie one way and mine another, and we may not meet again, you will ever be first in the heart of William Elliot."

He departed ; Mary disappeared ; and Hester sat down in the dark room they had left. " The sins of the fathers shall be visited on the children !" she murmured to herself. " Was it ever exemplified, in any case, more plainly than in this ? When

Matthew Goring made love to his daughter's governess, or encouraged her to make it to him—whichever it might be—outraging his wife, outraging his children, outraging me (I, who pointed out his wicked folly to him and got ridicule from him for my pains), did he imagine that very folly would be the means hereafter of destroying his dearest child's happiness and prospects in life? No. Yet it has proved so. Oh, men! you who have wives and children, how careful should you be to tread in the right path!"

Careful indeed! and Hester Halliwell is right. A little dereliction from it may seem but a light matter, not worth a thought, only worth the amusement of the moment, *and scarcely that:* it seemed but so to Dr. Goring. Yet for him what did it bring forth? His wife's destruction; his disgraceful second marriage; his own early death; the breaking-up of his children's home, and the driving them out, orphans, into the world. And now, as it seemed, the fatality was pursuing even them! Carelessly enough does man commit sin, but when on the point of wilfully falling into it, he would do well to pause and remember that the promises of God are never broken, and that one of those promises is, " I WILL VISIT THE SINS OF THE FATHERS UPON THE CHILDREN."

CHAPTER XI.

RIGHT AT LAST.

CHRISTMAS passed over, January passed over; and one morning in the first week in February it happened that Hester had business in town. Something arose, connected with the property of the Gorings, which rendered it necessary for her to seek an interview with the agent of Lawyer Stone, of Middlebury, who had made Dr. Goring's will. The agent was a Mr. Ecckington, living in the Temple; and Hester started by the omnibus, the first thing after breakfast. She got into the Temple—that is, into its mazes and windings—

and went about looking for Mr. Ecckington's
chambers, for she had never been there but
once, and did not readily remember the spot.
But she reached it at last: she knew it by a
neighbouring pump, whose handle was pad-
locked, and mounted the stairs, a great height,
for he lived on the top story.   She stood a
minute or two to recover breath—not being
able to run up seventy or eighty steps as
blithely as she once could—and then turned
the handle and knocked briskly at the black
door.   And after Hester had done that, lo!
and behold! there stood some great white
letters staring her in the face: "Serjeant
Pyne."

Serjeant Pyne was not Mr. Ecckington,
that was certain; but before Hester had time
to deliberate, a boy flung the door open.
She asked for Mr. Ecckington.

"In there," said the boy, opening an inside
door; and Hester entered the office.

She knew the room again directly, though its furniture was different, and she saw the tops of the pleasant green trees outside. A gentleman in a gray coat, with a pen behind his ear, rose from a desk and came forward.

"Sir," said Hester, "I am in search of Mr. Ecckington."

"Mr. Ecckington! Oh, the former occupant here. He has removed, ma'am, to chambers in Lincoln's Inn."

The gentleman gave the address—indeed, took the trouble to write it on a card—and directed her the best way to go there. Hester thanked him for his civility, which she thought extremely condescending for a serjeant, though it occurred to her afterwards that he might be only the serjeant's clerk. Hester went away, blaming Lawyer Stone's negligence in not having informed her of the removal of his agent, but had only gained the pump when her steps came to a halt, for it flashed across her mind that the address and number in Lincoln's Inn, just written down for her, was that of Mr. William Elliot.

She toiled up the stairs again, when Serjeant Pyne (or his clerk) assured her the address was Mr. Ecckington's : he knew nothing of Mr. William Elliot.

Hester got into Lincoln's Inn, nearly losing herself, and to her dismay found that Mr. Ecckington was out. " Gone before the Master of the Rolls," the clerk said, "and might not be in till late." So all Hester could do was to go back home again and write to appoint an interview. She had proceeded but a few steps when she came in view of a young gentleman sailing towards her, in a gray wig and black gown, which flew out with the wind on all sides as he walked. It cannot be said but that Hester looked on the wearers of these gowns with considerable awe (possibly because she had never seen much of them), and as there appeared scarcely space on the pavement for her and the gown to pass each other, Hester turned off it to give place. Imagine her astonishment when the gentleman stopped and held out his hand. She drew back, believing he mistook her for someone else, and half dropped a curtsey in her humility.

Positively it was Lawyer Stone's son, Bob! And though Hester had nursed him many a time when he was a child, coaxed him, kissed him, and once (if it may now be confessed) whipped him, she hardly presumed to let her hand meet his in his new dignity.

" You were going to pass me," he said.

" How was I to know you in that fine plumage ?" asked Hester. " I thought it might be nothing less than a judge coming along, and stood aside to give him room. So you are called !"

"Oh, thank goodness, yes; the worry's over.   I'm precious glad of it."

"I went to the Temple to find Mr. Ecckington this morning and heard he had moved here," observed Hester.   "Your father ought to have informed me."

"Ecckington is in Elliot's old chambers—took them off his hands," replied Mr. Stone. "Elliot gave up the law and is going to travel.   He was red-hot for the Crimea, but now the war is over he would be a day too late for the fair there, so he is off somewhere else.   He is up to his ears in preparations for his departure, for he purposes being abroad for years, if not for the term of his natural life—as the Bench says by our transports. Hope it may be my luck to say it sometime."

"What is the cause of Mr. Elliot's going?"

"He is in tantrums with his governor. The old folks put a stopper on his marriage with—— I declare, Miss Halliwell, I beg your pardon ! I forgot for the moment how nearly you were connected with the affair. I suppose you know more than I can tell you."

" Indeed, I know very little, beyond the fact that he and my niece are separated, Robert." (Hester brought the name "Robert" out with difficulty : it seemed too familiar so to address a personage in a wig and gown. Though, indeed, she used to call him nothing but "Bob.")

" They first, Sir Thomas and the old lady," continued he, in irreverent barrister fashion, " retracted their consent to the marriage, and then wormed an undertaking out of Elliot not to marry without. Which was like what the school-children say to their companions, when they have a cake from home and want to gormandize it all to their own cheek : 'Them as ask shan't have any ; and them as don't, don't want any.' "

The barrister laughed, and so did Hester.

In spite of his fine gown, he was Bob Stone still.   It set her more at ease.

"So Elliot gave his word, and of course will stick to it," he resumed ; " but afterwards, when he came to reflect upon the thing in cool blood, he felt that he had been harshly dealt by—tricked, in short, into promising away what we may call the subject's right of liberty.   Altogether, he was disgusted with everything, threw up his profession, and means to throw up Old England.   Good-morning, Miss Halliwell.   I'll tell the governor of his negligence when I write to Middlebury."

Now, it may sound (Hester remarked so afterwards) like a made-up incident, such as those we read of in a romance, to state that soon after parting with Mr. Stone she met William Elliot.   But it was so.   She was standing in the great thoroughfare, looking out for the right omnibus, when he came tearing along, pushing straight forward and looking at no one, in as much bustle as if he had all the business of the city on his shoulders. Hester caught his arm to stop him. He looked ill and careworn : her heart ached to see him.

"What is this I hear, William, about you quitting England ?"

"Why remain in it ?" was his answer. "What have I left to look forward to ?"

"Your profession," faltered Hester.

"I have lost interest in it. Men strive to get on, not only to attain eminence, but to win a home. They think of a wife ; of children ; of domestic happiness. They may gain the very highest honours of the land, but, without ties of the home and heart, such distinctions are cold and valueless. So I abandon a country where hope is denied me."

"This must be as a death-blow to your father and mother!" exclaimed Hester.

"A blow I believe it is.   I wish fate had been kinder to all of us."

"When do you go?"

"I leave London to-morrow night for Southampton.   The steamer for Malta starts the following day.   I visit the East first."

"To remain abroad—how long?"

"Probably for ever.   Certainly for years."

"Oh, William!" exclaimed Hester, "if I could only persuade you to relinquish your purpose!"

He smiled—a sickly smile.

"As others have sought to persuade me— ineffectually.   How is it at home?   Well?"

"Not very well," replied Hester, knowing to whom he alluded.   "Men can wear out regrets with bustle and travel, as you are about to do; but women, who are condemned to inactivity, retain remembrance more keenly."

"God be with you, dear Miss Halliwell!"

he said, preparing to move on ; "and take my dearest love and blessing to *her*. I dare say I shall never see either of you again."

He wrung her hand, in his emotion, till she thought he would have wrung it off; and a ring, which she happened to have on, cut right into her finger. But Hester was too much troubled to care for the pain. It seemed to her that Sir Thomas Elliot and his wife had much to answer for.

That same night Hester walked about her bedroom until the small hours of the morning. She was debating a question with herself. What *right*, human or divine, had Sir Thomas and Lady Elliot, in their obstinate pride and prejudice, to condemn two of their fellow-creatures to despair, even though one was the son to whom they had given birth? Did it not lie in her duty to point out to them their sin—to make an effort to awaken their own minds to it?

Firmer and firmer became Hester's conviction that it was so; and when her mind was
at length made up, a feeling came over her
that neither her own strength nor her own
spirit was urging her to it.

There was no time to let the grass grow
under her feet, and the next afternoon found
Hester at Sir Thomas Elliot's. Lady Elliot
was pitiably subdued by sorrow, and would
have given her own life to keep her son in
England. Hester entered upon the matter,
giving her opinion unshrinkingly; but Lady
Elliot was blind to all sides of the case save
her own, and spoke up, passionately com-
plaining.

"No joy have I had in life; no peace;
nothing but despair: before one affliction
yielded to time, another arose. I had nothing
left but him; nothing else to comfort me on
the wide earth; and now he is going away
for ever, for he is resolved not to return to

England. To-night he comes to take his leave, and I shall see him for the last time."

"And thankful I am, ma'am, that I am not in your shoes," said Hester. "If that young man decamps into unknown regions, amongst infidels and Hottentots, and rushes into sin and everything that's bad, to drown his unhappiness, you and his father must answer for it to his Maker, for you alone will have driven him to it."

"Oh, of course, of course," she answered, in tones of the bitterest sarcasm; "it has been my fault through life—everything; nobody's but mine. I wish it was ended!"

"I think a great deal has been your fault, Lady Elliot," rejoined Hester. "Various afflictions have come to you, *as they come to all,* and yours have not been worse than many others are. But have you striven to avert them, to turn them away? Have you been patiently submissive under them, and, accepting them as chastisements sent by God, resigned yourself fully to His good will? Have you endeavoured to make sunshine out of the blessings they have been mixed with?"

"What blessings?" asked Lady Elliot. "I know of none."

Hester gazed at her in surprise. The fact was, Lady Elliot had so accustomed herself to living a life of repining, that her mind was perverted, and she could see no good in anything.

"Does your ease count for nothing, your freedom from the cares of the world, your luxurious home?" cried Hester, as she directed her eyes round the room. "Do you forget the ample means you possess of gratifying every imaginable wish, and the golden opportunities afforded you of bestowing a tithe of your superfluous wealth upon those steeped in poverty? Above all, ma'am, do you reflect how rich you are in your son? What good gifts are there, whether of person or of mind, that have not been dealt out to him with an unsparing hand ? No blessings, Lady Elliot !"

" I *was* blest in him," she answered, " I was, I was ! And I shall be so no more."

" Oh, Lady Elliot, how blest you might still be !" uttered Hester. " Believe me, God's mercies are given to you *abundantly.* If you could but see them ! If you would but consent to tear the scales from your mind and convert its gloom into sunshine ! Did it ever occur to you to ask what children are bestowed on us for ?"

" For our punishment," perversely answered Lady Elliot. " Mine have been."

" They were bestowed on us that we might promote their happiness here, and so lead them to heaven through their gratitude, their thankfulness of heart," said Hester. " Not that we might selfishly crush their innocent hopes and thwart their wishes, at our own caprice or pleasure, driving them into rebellion, and so on to deceit, recklessness and evil."

"Then, when my father opposed me in my wish to marry," Lady Elliot resumed, in almost sullen tones, "you would say he ought to have consented to it? Is that your argument? It is a new one."

"No, I hope such an argument is not mine. Your father was right. The objection was to Thomas Elliot: and it was not a frivolous chimera, as in your son's case. Mr. Freer thought he was not calculated to make you happy; and his worldly circumstances were against any marriage, for he possessed nothing. The error there lay with you, Lady Elliot. Your duty was to bow to your father's decision and submissively wait, hoping that time would subdue the objections. You and Thomas Elliot were both young enough."

"You seem to be pretty well acquainted with my family affairs, Miss Halliwell!"

"I am not a total stranger to them. I have been for some years intimate with the Thornycrofts of Coastdown, who are relatives of the Elliot family; and I was myself once on the point of marriage with your husband's cousin, the Reverend George Archer: but I think you have heard this before. I have had my sorrows in life, Lady Elliot, as fully as most people: sorrows of the heart, of the inward life, as also of the outer. But I have striven, by patient resignation, to make the best of them; and they are sorrows to me no more. Yours will pass away, if you so choose; and the world will become plea-sant to you—always remembering to walk in it as your probation to a better. Try it, Lady Elliot."

"Try what?"

"To make your own happiness; to make

your husband's, *which you have never yet
heartily striven to do ;* to make your son's.
You will live to thank me for having suggested it."

Lady Elliot burst into tears and laid her
head on the sofa cushion.   And at that
moment Sir Thomas Elliot appeared at the
door and stood quietly rooted to it, in surprise.   Lady Elliot, from her position, could
not see him, and Hester pretended not to.
She thought it well that he should hear a bit
of her mind, as well as his wife.

"William is going forth into exile," she resumed to Lady Elliot, "a lonely, miserable
man : he voluntarily separates himself from
you.   Would he do this if you were true to
him, a loving mother ?   And you, what will
remain to you after his departure ?   Discon-
tented repining, bitter self-reproach, a yearn-
ing for him whom you cannot then bring
back.   You say that a curse—though, I

assure you, I shrink from repeating such a word—has followed you through life, follows you still. Break it, Lady Elliot !"

Lady Elliot raised her head and looked at Hester.

"Keep William by you, a son to rejoice in and be proud of. Let him make his own happiness and help him in it : take an interest in his plans, in his profession, and be to him a tender friend. Diffuse a pleasant spirit in your home : make the best of poor Clara, and win back the affections of your husband, as you strove to win them in your girlhood : and, above all, cherish in your heart a spirit of thankfulness to ONE who has put all these blessings in your way, a repentant, submissive, hopeful spirit—and none were ever submissive to Him in vain. Where would the curse be then ? Gone, Lady Elliot."

"If I could think—if I could think it has been, in a measure, my own fault, in thus

encouraging a murmuring spirit of rebellion !"
she wailed, clasping her hands in intense
anguish. "Oh! if I *could* change this black
despair for peace! If I could indeed retain
William at my side! If I could find happiness in what has been a thankless home!"

"I'll help you," cried Sir Thomas, coming
forward. "If you will only manage to keep
William in his own country and give us a bit
of cheerfulness at home, instead of gloom, I
will do my part towards it."

He looked, as he spoke, more like the
merry Tom Elliot of her girlhood than he
had done for years. Hope leaped up into
Hester's heart; she thought she saw her way
becoming clear, and she explained the purport
of her visit to Sir Thomas.

"In point of family, Mary Goring's is not
inferior to yours; and you and I, Sir Thomas,
only narrowly escaped being cousins in early
life."

"Through George Archer, the booby!" uttered Sir Thomas. "You would have saved him, Miss Halliwell."

"And—you will pardon me for stating it, Sir Thomas—when I and George Archer were once jestingly comparing notes as to our relative importance, my family, in point of descent and connections, was found to be superior to his and yours. Believe me, though you have risen in the world, Mary Goring's descent is equal to William Elliot's."

"But it was not Miss Goring's family we objected to," returned the knight.

"Oh yes, it was, in reality," said Hester. "Again I say, excuse my speaking freely, Sir Thomas; the subject justifies it. You and Lady Elliot were mortified because William did not choose a wife from the higher ranks of life. You stated to me, Sir Thomas, that, personally, you estimated Miss Goring highly."

" I do," he answered.

" And you cannot, you, a sensible man, believe that Dr. Goring was guilty. It is impossible that you can do so, if you have dispassionately examined into the details of the affair. Imprudent he was; infatuated; nothing more—and he paid the penalty. Do you think, if he had indeed committed a crime so awful and upon my own sister, that I would come here to excuse him, to protest there was no stain on his character? No, Sir Thomas. I have my own high and responsible duties in life to perform; and I would not say or do a thing that my conscience disapproves. When I assert Matthew Goring's innocence, I assert what I believe to be as true as that there is a heaven above us."

He made no reply.

" Think not I come here, as a petitioner, to urge my niece's claims, or to protest against her wrongs. Though the wrong, allow me to say, Lady Elliot, was forced upon her by your side, not sought on mine, for it was you who deliberately suffered the intimacy between her and William to grow up."

Sir Thomas nodded his head approvingly. No danger that he would gainsay that.

" No," resumed Hester, " I came here with no selfish motives, but because it was essential that someone should point out to you both how grievously you were erring; and I believed the task was allotted to me. To drive William away from his country and destroy his prospects in life, is a heavy sin to lay to your door. How will you atone for it ?"

Sir Thomas Elliot began pacing the room with uneasy strides. Presently he spoke, but in a reluctant tone.

" Since I first heard of the affair at Middlebury, I have learnt more of its particulars.

And I confess I now think it probable that
Dr. Goring was—so far as regarded his
wife's death—an innocent man."

"Then act upon it, Sir Thomas," cried
Hester briskly. "Stop your son's voyage
now, at the eleventh hour, and restore things
to their former footing."

"Louisa, what do you say?" he asked of
his wife. "I told you, once before, that in
this affair I would abide by your decision."

"I do not know what to say," sobbed Lady
Elliot. "If I could think——"

"Think that you are going to be happier
than you have been for many years," interrupted Hester. "Think that your dear son,
whom you grieve as lost to you, will remain
at home to comfort you with his love : think
of the merry romps you will have with his
children : and when the time arrives that you
are laid on your dying bed, Lady Elliot,
think that he will be at its side to bless you,

instead of beyond your reach, hundreds of
miles, over the salt sea."

She rose from the sofa, and the tears were
streaming down her cheeks, as she held out
her hand to Hester. " Miss Halliwell, you
have conquered. Thomas," she added, turning to her husband, "we may have done
wrong to William. Let us repair it."

" With all my heart," he replied. " Anything is preferable to the gloom which has
latterly overhung the house. Miss Halliwell,
we have to thank you for this. But if we
are really to turn over a new leaf and look
out for—what was it ?—sunbeams, you must
come often and repeat your lessons ; otherwise, we may forget the way and lapse back
again."

" Oh yes, I will be sure to come. But I do
not think you will do that now. And I
assure you, Sir Thomas Elliot, I never felt so .
proud in my life. To think that my poor,

homely pleading has effected this great purpose! But it was not mine. There was
ONE, greater than we are, who put it in my
heart to come, and has helped me through
with it."

They pressed Hester to stay to—she did
not hear whether it was tea or dinner. The
latter, she thought; but if so, it must have
been kept waiting a considerable time, for it
was long past seven o'clock. Not she. She
was too anxious to reach home and impart
the joyful news to Mary Goring.

Sir Thomas sat down by his wife as
Hester left the room.

" I will do my part towards it all, Loo," he
whispered : " on the old faith of Tom Elliot.
Here's my hand upon it."

She smiled pleasantly, and put her hand
into his.

" Oh, Thomas," she said, " we have both
been wrong, all these years—I see it all—

and I more wrong than you. Let us forget
and forgive and try to make life pleasant to
each other."

His smile echoed hers, and he leaned
forward and kissed her. The first happy
smile, the first voluntary kiss, they had ex-
changed for years.

" I think it seems as if the curse were
gone," she murmured, the rich glow of hope
lighting her cheek.

" I never believed there was one," smiled
Sir Thomas, " except in your imagination.
What may have seemed like it we brought
daily upon ourselves."

" By not making the best of things," she
eagerly answered. " Oh yes : it was so."

As Hester was passing the dining-room
door, Clara Elliot saw her, and, with a
scream of delight, ran out, jumping around
her like a little dog. Poor child ! her mind
was no stronger. But of that there was no

hope.   Miss Graves looked out also, very much astonished to see who was the visitor. Hester did not explain.

"Why do I never go to your house?" Clara exclaimed. "It is such a long while ! Why don't you send Mary to see me?"

"Mary has been very ill, my dear," answered Hester. "She cannot go out now."

"Mary ill! Let me come and see her to-morrow."

"Yes, dear child, you shall," interrupted Lady Elliot, advancing. "And I will go with you. Oh, Miss Halliwell!" she whispered, shaking Hester once more by the hand, "I think you are right. You don't know what a load is taken off my heart!"

As Hester left the street-door, who should be stepping out of a cab but William Elliot. She waited while he paid the cabman, and then took him by surprise.

"I have just left your father and mother."

" Indeed !" he said, looking almost incredulous. " This is my farewell evening with them, Miss Halliwell. I go down by the night train."

" So you persist in leaving England ?"

" I sail to-morrow."

" Now, which would you rather do, Mr. William ?" cried she. " Go abroad in that horrid steamer—no disparagement to it in particular, but all steamers are horrid—from which you will wish yourself out again before you have been a couple of hours at sea, or stop at home and marry Mary Goring ?"

" Oh," he evasively answered, while the red colour flushed into his face, " I am so overwhelmed with preparations for the start, that I can think of nothing else just now."

" But just ask yourself the question : *and answer it as you will.*"

There was something in Hester's tone which struck upon him, even more forcibly than the words. He grasped her by the shoulder—what *did* she mean?

" Go in, dear William," whispered Hester. " I have paved the way for you with Sir Thomas and Lady Elliot. I think if you do prefer Mary to the steamer, you may have her."

Hester never knew whether she reached home on her head or her heels. A dilatory omnibus, given to stopping, took her, but she herself was not clear upon the point. Lucy exclaimed at her long absence, and inquired if she had taken tea.

" No. I should like a cup."

She took a light and went upstairs to the best bedroom, which had been given up to Mary for the illness which had followed the breaking of her engagement. She had fallen into a doze, as she lay on the sofa. Quietly taking off her own cloak and bonnet, Hester sat down by her. Nothing of Mary could be seen but her face, for she had wrapped a shawl round her and someone had thrown a covering over her feet. Her brow was contracted as with pain, and her mouth stood slightly open—often the case in illness—but the young face, in spite of its whiteness, was lovely still.

" We will soon have that fair brow smooth again, my child," thought Hester, as she gently stirred the fire into a blaze.

Presently Hester heard a noise as of talking, downstairs. It mounted to the drawing-room adjoining ; and then Lucy appeared, carrying the cup of tea. But Hester rose from her seat in amazement, for stealing in after her was William Elliot.

" The idea of his coming down to-night," thought Hester. " And how quickly he must have followed upon me !"

" I could not help it," Lucy whispered to her in a tone of apology. " He would see

Mary, and when I urged that she was in her bedroom, he said what did that matter? Oh, Hester! he says she is to be his wife, after all!"

The bustle woke Mary, and the hectic flushed into her cheek when consciousness fully returned to her. She would have risen up, but William Elliot prevented it. He was shocked to terror at the change he saw in her, and, as he told Hester afterwards, believed her to be dying. He leaned over her with gentle tenderness, and his hot tears fell on her face.

"Oh, Mary!" he whispered, as he laid his cheek to hers; "I see how ill you have been, but you must bear up, for my sake. Our separation is over, my darling: my mother will be here to-morrow to tell you so. Very soon, very soon, you will be all mine."

"But what about the steamer, William?"

asked Hester in the gladness of her heart, but making believe to be very serious.

" The steamer must go without me."

" But your preparations—your outfit and your great strong boxes ? Are they to be wasted ?"

" I will give them to you if you like, Aunt Hester," quoth he. " I am in a generous mood."

" And go back to the law again ?" she questioned.

" Of course. Hoping, in time, to lord it over you all on the woolsack. Who knows but I may ?"

Hester snatched a moment to drink her tea. Mary, always thirsty now, glanced at it with eager eyes. Then William Elliot pleaded for some, to put him in mind of old times, he said, and convince him he was not dreaming. Next, Lucy thought she should like a cup, instead of supper. So they had the round table drawn before Mary's sofa, and actually, as Hester expressed it, held a tea-party in the bedroom. She said she hoped no one would reproach her with its being improper. When Frances Goring came in from the schoolroom to say good-night, there they were seated at it, with a great plate of buttered toast before them ; and Frances looked as if she never meant to recover from her astonishment. She stood just inside the room, staring at William Elliot.

" Ah, Frances! how do you do ?" he said, holding out his hand.

But Miss Frances, like the schoolgirl she was, stood immovable.

" What have you come again for, Mr. Elliot ?" she brought out.

" I ? To have another of your aunt's housekeeping lessons," he merrily answered. " Touching the apple-tarts and legs of mutton, you know. She must give it to me especially, to-night. Mary is too ill."

"And are you coming again — other nights ?"

" I hope so."

" Oh !" cried Frances, clasping her hands, " I am so glad ! It seems like those famous evenings back again. If you could only make Mary well, as she was then !"

" I'll try to," said William Elliot.

Hester went downstairs with him when he was leaving.

"You see how ill she looks," whispered Hester. " Do not set your heart too steadfastly upon her."

" Change of prospects will do much for her," was his reply ; " and change of air may do the rest. She shall have that with me."

"With you, Mr. William !"

"Yes. And you know what that must imply," he returned, with a smile of very

decided meaning. "So, if the former preparations are done away with, dear Miss
Halliwell, you had best set about some more
with morning dawn. We have suffered too
much to risk another separation, and I
promise you that, ill or well, Mary Goring
shall soon be Mary Elliot."

Lady Elliot came the next day and burst
into tears when she saw Mary: like her son,
she was deeply shocked. Clara would not
go away again, so Lady Elliot left her to
remain a day or two.

However, as William Elliot had said,
change of prospects seemed to do wonders
for Mary. Her recovery was rapid, not all
at once to robust health, but sufficiently so
to remove their fears. The wedding was
fixed for the last week in April. Hester was
for deferring it until the Midsummer holidays,
when the house would be free and Mary

stronger, but Mr. Elliot banteringly inquired
if she would not prefer to defer it till Midsummer two years. And the Rev. Alfred
Halliwell took a long journey across the
country to marry them, as he had once before
taken a journey to marry her unfortunate
mother. He was going to allow himself a
fortnight's holiday, that is, from the Monday
till the next Saturday week, a friend taking
his duty for him on the intervening Sunday,
and Mr. Dewisson's curate taking it on
the week-days. Previously to this, his son
George had sailed again as third officer, in
a far better ship and service than the
last.

They had a jolly wedding, as Master
Alfred Goring expressed it. Lady Elliot
was in a dazzling dress of satin and gold,
which caused every eye in the church to
water, and threw Mary's white silk quite into
the shade. Frances Goring was bridesmaid,

thereby acquiring an unlimited amount of vanity, which she has not lost yet.

Hester never could tell how she comported herself at the breakfast-table, excepting that it was very badly. She took the top of the table, having Sir Thomas Elliot on her right hand and Mr. Pepper, a gray-haired gentleman, in gold spectacles and heavy gold chain, on her left. The clergyman was at the foot of the table, having the bride and bridegroom on one side of him and Lady Elliot on the other. Sir Thomas made merry over Hester's nervous mistakes and kept everyone alive with laughter. He seemed quite to have returned to the free and open manners of his youth ; and Hester felt certain that he *was* doing his part of the bargain, as he had promised Lady Elliot. It is probable they both felt, as they looked around, that Mary Goring's connections were not so very despicable, after all, or so far removed from their own

position. Looking down upon the numerous
guests was the portrait of Mary's ancestor,
the Lady Hester Halliwell. Wonderfully,
with years, had Hester grown like it.
Strangers, calling, often thought it was
Hester's portrait, and that she had dressed
herself in the old style of George the Second
to have it taken. Lady Elliot looked happy
too—really happy, as Hester had never seen
her look until lately. Miss Graves was in
high feather, and sat next to Master Alfred,
whom she kept in order, at the request of
Hester. She had not gone to church, having
remained with Clara, for they had not ventured to take the latter. Poor Clara! she was
dressed out as splendidly as her mother,
laughed, by starts, all breakfast-time, and
nearly had one of her eating-fits, but William
Elliot had her by his side and restrained her.
Jessie Pepper and little Jane Goring were
also at the table : as to the other pupils and

the teachers, they had holiday and a handsome dinner ; so everyone was pleased and the day passed off delightfully.

They left early in the afternoon, the bride and bridegroom, in one of Sir Thomas Elliot's carriages, for the London Bridge Station, intending to reach Dover that evening and France the following day ; purposing to remain on the Continent all the summer, and perhaps the autumn. " It will benefit Mary," William Elliot had said, " and we both deserve a holiday." Meanwhile, Lady Elliot and Hester had promised to occupy themselves with the furnishing and arranging of their new residence, Mr. Elliot especially charging Hester to see to the setting-up of the housekeeping department. Hester was the last to shake hands with him in the hall, whilst Sir Thomas was handing Mary to the carriage.

" You will take care of her, William ?"

whispered Hester, the tears falling from her eyes, and she calling them "tiresome" for it. "She cannot be said to be well yet."

"You know there is no need to give me the injunction." William Elliot answered, whilst the ingenuous flush stole into his face, the sweet, earnest look to his truthful eye. "When I bring Mary home again, she will be so improved you will none of you recognise her." And Hester felt that his words were likely to be verified.

Late in the evening, when all had dispersed, the two sisters and their brother sat around the fire. They had not so sat, alone, for many, many years. "And," Mr. Halliwell said, remarking upon it, "we may never so sit again."

Hester told him the story of Lady Elliot, how she had been aroused from her grum-

bling and sinful discontent : that very day
she had again fervently thanked Hester for
awaking her to hope and to peace in life.

"She should have had half the trials to
endure that have fallen to my lot," exclaimed
the clergyman.

"Do you know what I have often thought
of?" remarked Lucy, "often and often. That
theory of Aunt Copp's—that because our
father heedlessly risked his money and lost
it, not because he was poor, but to increase
his riches when he had already plenty,
leaving us almost destitute, we, his children,
should have to wrestle with hard fate through
life. Do you remember her saying it, Alfred ?
do you, Hester ?"

They nodded.

"It has proved tolerably true with most of
us," said Mr. Halliwell. "But God has been
very good to us, for—thanks be unto Him !

—our trials might have been so much worse ; and lately they have been considerably lessened. Sorrows are the necessary evils of mortality, but we can well endure them when we look to that blessed land of rest which they are fitting us for. Many whose outward lot is cast in brightness make sorrow for themselves. Look at what you say of Lady Elliot."

"Oh yes," interrupted Hester ; "indeed, we have MUCH to be thankful for. Brighter days are come upon us all than we once hoped for ; and I trust our hearts have been so purified that we may 'endure to the end.' But I wish I could arouse the whole world to a healthy state of mind, as I was humbly instrumental in arousing that of Lady Elliot."

I wish she could. For let every one of God's creatures be fully assured that they possess within themselves the power to make or mar, in a great measure, their own happiness here; *that upon the state of the mind and heart depends life's sunshine.*

THE END.

BILLING AND SONS, PRINTERS, GUILDFORD.
J. D. & Co

www.ingramcontent.com/pod-product-compliance
Lightning Source LLC
Chambersburg PA
CBHW060532030726
47498CB00004B/1172